bright purple

bright purple

color me confused

melody carlson

Discipleship Inside Out™

NavPress is the publishing ministry of The Navigators, an international Christian organization and leader in personal spiritual development. NavPress is committed to helping people grow spiritually and enjoy lives of meaning and hope through personal and group resources that are biblically rooted, culturally relevant, and highly practical.

**For a free catalog go to www.NavPress.com
or call 1.800.366.7788 in the United States or 1.800.839.4769 in Canada.**

© 2006 by Melody Carlson

TH1NK and the TH1NK logo are a registered trademarks of NavPress. Absence of ® in connection with marks of NavPress or other parties does not indicate an absence of registration of those marks.

ISBN 978-1-57683-950-8

Cover design by studiogearbox.com
Cover image by Jack Hollingsworth/Getty
Creative Team: Nicci Hubert, Arvid Wallen, Erin Healy, Darla Hightower, Bob Bubnis

This is a work of fiction. The characters, incidents, and dialogues are products of the author's imagination and are not to be construed as real. Any resemblance to actual events or persons, living or dead, is entirely coincidental.

Published in association with the literary agency of Sara A. Fortenberry.

Carlson, Melody.
   Bright purple : color me confused / Melody Carlson. -- 1st ed.
      p. cm. -- (Truecolors series)
   Summary: When Ramona learns that her best friend since grade school is a lesbian, she struggles to decide how to respond, knowing that people of her community, and even her church, have trouble discussing homosexuality civilly.
   ISBN 1-57683-950-8
   [1. Best friends--Fiction. 2. Friendship--Fiction. 3. Lesbians --Fiction. 4. Homosexuality--Fiction. 5. High schools--Fiction. 6. Schools--Fiction. 7. Christian life--Fiction.]   I. Title.
   PZ7.C216637Bri 2007
   [Fic]--dc22

                                              2006016237

Printed in the United States of America

4 5 6 7 8 9 10 / 15 14

Other Books by Melody Carlson

one

My best friend just told me she's a lesbian. *A lesbian!*

Just like that, as we're sitting in the food court at the Greenville Mall, Jess calmly makes this little announcement, then adds, "I just thought you should know."

"Real funny." I roll my eyes at her and attempt to turn my attention back to my half-eaten veggie burrito. Jess and I have been best friends since grade school and she's always had this really wacky sense of humor. "Give me a break," I tell her. "Can't you see I'm trying to eat here?"

"I'm serious, Ramie."

"Yeah, right." But even as I try to brush her words away, my head begins to feel a little fuzzy, and for some strange reason my upper lip is starting to feel numb. I wonder if it's something I ate.

"I figured you'd act like this," she says. "I mean going into total denial."

"Quit messing with my mind," I tell her, avoiding her eyes. But at the same time, I can feel this thing way down deep in the pit of my stomach. And I'm getting totally freaked. Is it possible that she is really serious?

"I decided to come out of the closet," she continues in this aggravatingly offhanded way. Like this is no big deal, like people

7

make announcements like this every day. "And I need you to believe me, Ramie. Trust me, it's not easy to say this to you."

I force myself to look at her now. Her expression is dead serious and I'm pretty sure she's not joking. But at the same time, she doesn't really look quite like herself either. Something seems different, and I'm wondering, *Is this really the Jessica LeCroix that I grew up with? Or is this an impostor?* I mean can this really be the same girl who moved in down the street when we were in fourth grade? The girl who taught me how to play soccer and basketball? Can this possibly be the same girl I've shared secrets and sleepovers with? Oh sure, she has the same curly dark hair pulled back in a messy tail, those same dark, penetrating eyes, but something about her is different. Maybe it's just what she's told me. Can it really be true? Suddenly it's like I am scared. Really, really scared. I feel frightened of her. And this shockwave of reality shoots through me.

"Do you really mean this?" I manage to say in a raspy voice. My upper lip is so numb now that it feels like it's been shot with Novocain, and I actually reach up to touch it to see if it's still there. This is so freaky. So bizarre. Maybe it's just a bad dream.

Jess nods, her dark brows pulling together in a deep frown, and it almost looks like she's fighting to hold back tears.

"Jess?" I hear the strain in my voice as I stare at her, making this silent plea with my eyes, like, *tell me this isn't really happening.* Or that it's just a lame joke. Or wake me up and tell me that it's just a horrible nightmare.

She presses her lips together as if she's afraid to say another word. Then she looks down at the table and lets out a long sigh. "I'm sorry if you hate me now," she mutters. "But it's true."

And that's when I start to feel sick, really sick, like I'm-going-to-hurl sick, like I-better-get-out-of-here fast-sick.

"I gotta go," I blurt as I stand up and make a mad dash to the bathroom. I nearly knock down an old woman as I blast through the swinging door and race into the closest stall just in time to lose my lunch in the toilet. I close the door behind me, then remain in the stall as I attempt to catch my breath and ask myself what just happened. What is going on? What did Jess just tell me? Was it real or did I just imagine it because my burrito made me sick?

I lean my back against the cool metal door and blankly stare at the bright purple tiles that surround the toilet. I am trying to process what I've just heard. Trying to decide whether I'm losing my mind. It is possible that Jess is just pulling a fast one on me. Maybe she's trying to teach me a lesson, to get back at me for trying to match her up with Joey Pinckney last week. Okay, I'll admit I was just kidding. The kid is kind of nerdy, and some kids think he's gay, which I doubt, but I'd seen the two of them talking like they really were interested in each other. Who wouldn't tease about something like that?

"You left your purse at the table," she says from the other side of the door.

"Thanks," I mutter, still unable to emerge from my temporary shelter.

"You okay, Ramie?"

"Must've been that stupid burrito," I say as I flush the chunky remains down the toilet and suppress the urge to gag again. "Guess those beans had gone bad or something."

"Yeah, I've warned you about that restaurant. BJ still swears she got food poisoning from their fish tacos last month." Her voice sounds a little lighter now. As a result, I experience this faint flicker of hope, like maybe this really is just a hoax. Maybe it's like that *Tom Green Show* where people get scammed while the camera is running.

Gotcha! Maybe Jess is wearing a minicam right this minute and I'm going to be on TV next week.

"You were jerking me around out there, weren't you?" I say as I tear off a big strip of toilet paper and wipe my mouth, then loudly blow my nose. "You didn't really mean what you said, did you, Jess?"

No answer.

Suddenly I think of something that gives me this tiny twinge of hope. "I mean I've heard you making fun of those weird girls at school, Jess, the ones who kiss each other on the lips like it's no big deal. I've heard you saying that they're sick and just trying to get attention. Remember how we'd both say that they were disgusting freaks?"

Still no response.

"Jess?" I take in a deep breath, steadying myself to go out and face her now, to convince her that this is all just a really, really bad joke, but one that I won't hold against her—if we can simply forget the whole thing and go back to life as normal.

"I just wanted to be honest with you, Ramie. I thought it was about time I told you the truth about me."

I lean my head against the door with a dull thud, then tightly shut my eyes. How can this be? How could we have been just sitting there, happily eating our lunch, and then Jess announces that she's gay? Like who does that anyway? And how is it possible that I never even saw this coming? I mean if your best friend has no clue that you're gay, then who does? And how can you be sure that you really are gay? Furthermore, what does that suggest about me? I mean we've been best friends for years. Is it possible that Jess thinks maybe I'm gay too? That she and I can be lovers now? *Ugh!* I think I'm going to barf again.

Then a worse thought hits me. What if I actually am gay and don't even know it yet? Is that even possible? And what will our friends at school say when they find out about this? Or our friends at church for that matter? And how can Jess still be a Christian if she's a lesbian?

Way too many questions go racing around in circles through my head, until I am seriously dizzy. I feel like Dorothy in *The Wizard of Oz*, the scene where she's trapped in the little farmhouse that's being spun about by the tornado. Only I'm trapped in this bright purple cubicle that's whirling around and around as my entire life spins totally out of control. *Help me!*

two

"I CAN'T DEAL WITH THIS RIGHT NOW," I TELL JESS, TURNING AWAY FROM HER toward the row of sinks. I finally emerged from the whirling purple stall, but I'm afraid to leave the restroom just yet. Maybe I think I'm going to hurl again. Or maybe I just don't want anyone to see me — or more honestly, to see us — *together.* I glance at my reflection in the mirror above the sink, instantly trying to erase the expression of disgust that's carved into my forehead. *Try to look natural,* I tell myself as I smooth back some strands of my long dark hair, noticing that I'm due for some straightening again. *Try to act normal,* I think as I pretend to touch up my lip gloss with this new shade of Hot Cocoa that I just bought at Macy's. *Act as if stuff like this happens all the time.* Yeah, right.

"Sorry," Jess mutters from behind me. I can feel her watching me now. I wish she would just leave. Just leave me alone! Or maybe she could just vanish altogether.

"My mom is supposed to pick me up at two," I say as I run water and squirt some pink liquid soap onto my hands. This is a total lie, but it seems necessary. I know that I won't be able to ride home in Jess's car today. Or ever again, for that matter. The mere idea of being contained in such a small space with her for more than a few seconds makes me feel nauseous. I continue standing in front of the bathroom sink, washing and washing my hands, as if I've just turned into a germ-a-phobe or developed OCD or something. But the truth is I do feel slightly contaminated just now. I think it happened when my hand brushed against hers when she gave me my purse. It's as if I became defiled.

"*Why* is your mom picking you up?" Jess asks. I can hear the suspicion in her voice and it irritates me. Of course, I'm lying. Who wouldn't under these circumstances? But I continue just the same, digging my hole even deeper.

"I promised to help her find something for her friend's wedding," I say lightly. "Remember Janelle? She's getting married next month and I—"

"Yeah, okay." She throws a strap of her backpack over one shoulder, then walks toward the door. I continue washing my hands.

"Sorry," I say. "I guess I just kinda forgot."

"See ya then," she says.

"Yeah, see ya," I echo, knowing that I never want to see her again. I wish that I'd never met her. Wish that we'd never been friends. I turn off the faucet and feel hot tears coming down my cheeks now. I dry my hands and face on the rough paper towel and stare at myself in the mirror again. Why me? Why does something like this have to happen to me? These bright purple walls and florescent lighting make my normally bronze complexion look like a dark ashen gray, almost as if I'm dead. And that's just how I feel inside—*dead*—as if someone has just knifed me from behind and all the blood has drained out of my body and I am really not here at all. Walking dead.

Then a couple of girls I've never met come into the restroom, and I can feel them looking at me, giggling about some private joke. Maybe they know about Jess. Maybe they suspect that I am like her too. I turn and leave the restroom, hurrying away, looking for a place to escape to. But mostly, I look to see whether Jess is still hanging around, maybe looking for me, waiting to see whether my mom is really coming to get me, or if it was just a lie. Of course it was a lie. Get a clue, Jess!

But, feeling guilty for lying as well as desperate, I pull out my cell phone and call my mom.

"I thought you were with Jess," she says with some impatience.

"I was, Mom, but something came up," I tell her. "Kind of an emergency."

"Is everyone okay?"

"Yeah. But I need a ride, Mom. Or I suppose I could take the bus."

"No, no," she says quickly, just as I knew she would. My mom has this big phobia about me using mass-transit systems. She thinks someone is going to attack me or mug me or rape me or, perhaps worst of all, use some racial slur against me. And so we arrange for her to drive by and pick me up at Macy's west entrance.

"But I can't be there for about an hour," she tells me.

I complain a little, but she insists it's the best she can do.

"I'm sure you can find something to keep you busy," she tells me.

So, worried that I'll run into Jess again, I go into a certain store that she has always really, really loathed—Victoria's Secret. I wonder about this as I walk around the crowded store. (They're having their semi-annual sale this week.) I try to understand what exactly about women's underwear was so abhorrent to her as I pretend to examine a lacy bra that's about the same color as a yellow fire hydrant. I mean you'd think that a lesbian might get into a store like this, a place where lots of females are trying on skimpy undergarments and . . . Suddenly I feel sick to my stomach again. *What am I thinking?* It's hard to believe that Jess used to be my friend! My *best* friend! I lean over slightly, bracing myself against the big round table of size-36 bras as I take in a deep breath and attempt to erase these repulsive thoughts from my mind.

"Are you okay?" asks a concerned-looking sales clerk.

I stand up straight, still clutching the bright yellow bra. "Yeah," I say quickly. "I just felt kind of faint, you know. Probably low blood sugar or something."

She nods. "Did you want to try that on?" she asks, pointing to the bra still in my hands.

"Sure," I tell her, noticing that it really is a pretty good buy. "If you have it in a B cup."

So off she goes in search of the right size, and before long I am waiting in line to try it on, along with several other bras as well. This sales girl is good. She managed to find several more in styles she thought I might like—all in shockingly bright colors too. She must think I'm a bright freak. Oh well. I'm just killing time anyway, right? That and avoiding Jess. I can't imagine a safer place to do it. That is, unless Jess has been stalking me and is secretly hiding in here somewhere. I glance nervously down the hall in the waiting area. But I don't see her. To be honest, Jess would stand out in this crowd. Perhaps that's one reason I always assumed she never liked shopping here. Jess is not exactly fat, but she is thick and wide and stocky. Great for a soccer goalie, but a store like this doesn't exactly stock her size. Besides that, she pretty much sticks to sports bras. I figured that was why she avoided this store. But maybe I was wrong. Maybe her aversion was something more.

I study the women and girls who are waiting in line ahead of me. I wonder if any of them are lesbians. Do any of them have lesbian friends? And how does a person deal with such things anyway? It hurts my head to think about it. Finally, I go into the softly lit room; I think the dim light is supposed to make the bras or your body look better. I take my time as I try on the vibrant selection, and to my surprise the fire-hydrant one seems to fit perfectly.

By the time I wait in line to purchase it, it's almost time for my mom to get here. Keeping my head down, I hurry down the mall toward Macy's. But when I'm about halfway there, I question this. Why should I have to keep my head down and act like I'm ashamed? I'm not the one who's made the shocking announcement. I have nothing to hide. But even as I tell myself this, I am not convinced. I know how people are, how they think. As soon as word gets out about Jess's sexual orientation, I will be implicated. Guilty by association. My life is over.

three

"WHAT WAS THE BIG EMERGENCY?" MOM ASKS AS I CLIMB INTO HER VOLVO and slam the door behind me. "Did something happen to Jess?"

I try to laugh that one off. "Yeah, I guess you could say that."

"What?" She turns and looks at me with arched brows. "Is she okay?"

"That depends on how you define *okay*."

"What?" demands my mom. "What is the matter with Jess?"

My mom and I have this unusually open relationship. Some kids assume it's because my mom is pretty young for a mom, but I think it's mostly because it's just me and mom — my dad split a long time ago. But it's also possible that this closeness is due to the fact that she's Caucasian and I'm biracial. As a result, she has spent a lot of time talking to me and counseling me, trying to prepare me for all the "challenges" that she has always assumed would come my way. Fortunately, my challenges (well, until today) have not been all that challenging.

"Do you really want to know?" I ask her, unsure if I can actually say these words out loud.

"Of course I want to know, Ramie. What is wrong with Jess?" Mom stops for a red light, then suddenly turns and peers at me with wide blue eyes. "She's not pregnant, is she?"

"*Mom!*" But even as I act shocked by her question, I'm thinking it would be highly preferable, at least to me, if Jess *was* pregnant. I seriously think I could deal with something like that.

"Well, you know me. Since I got pregnant when I was only twenty, well, I suppose I just have some natural paranoia about that sort of thing."

"Yeah, Mom, believe me, *I know.*" Like how many lectures have I had on this subject? Not that she should be worried. I made an abstinence pledge years ago, and I have no intentions of backing out of it anytime soon. Of course, my mom, who is not a Christian, doesn't really get this. And I suppose that's the reason she always feels like she has to be on her guard about these things.

"So." Mom sighs as she proceeds across the intersection. "That's a relief. But tell me, Ramie, what *is* wrong with Jess? Did she get in trouble with her parents over something? What's up? Tell me."

"It's just so horrible," I begin, trying to think of some way to say this thing, some way to get the words out without starting to feel physically ill all over again.

"What is it, Ramie?" says Mom with real sympathy. "Oh, please don't tell me that Jess is—is sick. One of my clients just found out her son has leukemia, the really bad kind. Oh, please tell me that Jess doesn't have—"

"No!" I snap at my mom. "She does not have cancer."

"Oh good." Mom sighs again. "So, what is it then?"

Okay, God forgive me, but I'm thinking I'd prefer that Jess *did* have cancer. Not something as serious as my mom's client's son, of course. And I do feel bad about this. I know it just shows that I'm a selfish and horrible person, but at least they have cures for cancer nowadays, don't they? But can anyone cure gay?

"Jess is a lesbian!" I blurt.

My mom is quiet for about a minute, as if she is taking this in. "Well, that's not so bad, Ramie."

"Not so bad?" I practically scream. "Jess is—rather, she *was*—my best friend. We have been best friends for like . . . like, forever! How can she possibly be a lesbian?"

Mom just nods, like she's still processing this news flash. But I can tell she's not greatly disturbed by it. I'm sure this is because of two things. (1) She's a family counselor, so she's "seen it all," and (2) She is *not* a Christian, and she thinks homosexuality is all okay. Well, fine. A lot of good it did for me to dump on her like this. I turn away from her and glare out the passenger's side window. I can't believe my best friend does something like this and then my mom takes her side. Why couldn't I have had a Christian parent? Someone who gets me?

Then it occurs to me that Jess *does* have Christian parents, strong Christian parents! It was probably mostly due to their influence, and Jess's too, that I ever started going to church in the first place and, consequently, that I gave my heart to the Lord when I was twelve. I remember how happy her family was for me. I can also recall about a year later when Mr. LeCroix took Jess and me out for ice-cream sundaes, shortly after we signed our abstinence pledges at church, and I remember how he gave us both our True Love Waits rings. I twist the thin band of gold around my finger and wonder how Jess's parents are going to handle this. Maybe they won't. Maybe Mr. LeCroix will put his foot down and forbid it. Maybe he will tell Jess that she cannot be gay, that the Bible will not allow it, and that will be the end of this whole miserable business. Oh, if only life were that simple.

"Ramie." My mom says my name in that tone that suggests that she's been talking and I haven't been listening.

"Huh?"

"I was just telling you that you're going to have to deal with this."

"Deal with it?"

"Yes. You need to accept that Jessica is homosexual. And it's not her fault; it's just the way she is. People are born that way, Ramie. And the sooner you can accept this, the sooner you can help her with—"

"Help *her?*" I turn and stare at my mother.

She nods. "Yes. Jessica is going to need help with this, Ramie. It's not easy telling people about your sexual orientation. It was very brave of her to come out to you. That shows she really trusts you, but more than ever right now she needs her friends to support—"

"Forget it!" I firmly shake my head. "I am *not* her friend, Mom. Not anymore. If Jess wants to be a lesbian, well fine, that's her stupid choice and I don't have to—"

"It's *not* a choice, Ramie."

"Says who?"

"Says most of the experts, dear. You don't treat it—"

"Just because some stupid shrinks say homosexuality is okay and that people are born that way, which I seriously doubt anyone can prove, does *not* mean that God says it's okay. The Bible makes that pretty clear, Mom."

"Not everyone happens to believe that, sweetie." She turns and smiles at me with that patronizing expression she likes to wear when we don't agree on something that has to do with religion or the Bible. I'm sure this is only because she was raised by my very uptight and overly religious grandparents. They think *everything* is a sin. And they've never gotten over her having a baby "out of wedlock," not to mention a mixed-race baby as well. In other words, my know-it-all counselor mom has her own issues.

"You mean not everyone believes the Bible?" I ask for clarification. "Because that's like *duh*, Mom. I know that some people don't believe the Bible. I'm just saying that I—"

"No, that's not what I meant, Ramie. I'm trying to say that not even all Christians believe homosexuality is wrong. For instance, I have a client right now who is openly gay. And I happen to know that he and his partner were married in a church."

"Not a Christian church," I counter.

"Yes, it was," she insists. "And he said it was a fairly traditional Christian church. I can't recall what denomination."

"Well, it was probably some weirdo, kinky kind of church. Not like the church where I go."

"And where Jessica goes."

"*Used* to go."

"You mean they won't allow her to go there if she's a lesbian?"

I consider this. "I guess I don't really know for sure. But I do know they'll think that it's a sin. I'm sure they will."

"Well, I'll never understand that," she says as she pulls into the garage that's attached to our townhouse.

"What?"

"How churches can turn their backs on people like that. People in need."

"I didn't say that," I tell her as we get out.

She just shakes her head as she reaches into the backseat for her briefcase. "It was implied, Ramie. And besides, I've seen it enough times before. I know that it happens. And *that* is one of the main reasons you won't catch me going to church." She closes the door with a bang. "People who live in glass houses should not throw stones!"

I want to ask her what that's supposed to mean, but I am too frustrated to speak right now. And I sure don't want another lecture.

Okay, I realize that Mom and I don't agree on everything. But this is probably one of the biggest things we've ever disagreed on before. I really do feel betrayed. Sure, she might think that homosexuality is just fine for Jess, but what about me? Can't she see how Jess's decision is impacting me? What am I supposed to do with that? My mom might be a counselor, but she is clueless when it comes to helping her own daughter.

four

JESS AND I USUALLY GO TO YOUTH GROUP TOGETHER ON SATURDAY NIGHTS.
But I have no intention of going there with her tonight. Although,
after her big revelation today, I wonder whether she will actually
go. I mean wouldn't she be worried that I might tell someone? That
the word will get out and everyone will be whispering behind her
back, avoiding her, treating her like she has cooties? Seriously, how
embarrassed would she be if our youth group knew?

Unless this is all just part of her whacked-out plan. Maybe she
took some kind of coming-out class, like How to Destroy Your Life
in One Easy Lesson. What if she plans to show up at youth group
and come out of the closet in front of God and everyone tonight? If
that's the case, I'd just as soon lay low. I do *not* want to be around to
witness something so freaky. I've had enough stress already today.

But around six o'clock I begin to question this decision. I mean
why should I allow Jess's craziness to drive me away from *my* chance
for fellowship? And just when I happen to need it most! I have as
much right to be there as she does. In fact, in light of her recent
disclosure, I might even have more. At least I haven't chosen a devi-
ant and sinful lifestyle. So at six thirty, after polishing off some left-
over spaghetti, I decide to call BJ. She's a close friend of both mine
and Jess's, and I wonder if she's heard the latest.

"This is Ramie," I say to Mrs. Trestle as I put my empty bowl into the dishwasher. "Is BJ there?"

"Bethany Jane!" her mom calls out. "Ramie wants to speak to you."

I listen to the silence for a few seconds. "Hey, Ramie," says BJ. "What's up?"

I can tell by the upbeat tone of her voice that she doesn't know about Jess yet. "I, uh, I wondered if I could catch a ride with you to youth group tonight," I say. "I mean if you're going. Are you?"

"Yeah, sure. I was just about to leave. But don't you usually ride with Jess? Is she sick or something?"

"I . . . uh. . . . I'm not really sure."

"Are you okay, Ramie? You sound kinda weird."

"It's been a hard day," I admit. "Maybe I can tell you about it later."

"Sure. I'll pick you up in about fifteen."

"Cool."

So I make a quick dash up to my room, change into a hot pink turtleneck sweater that my mom thinks looks really great on me, put on some silver hoop earrings, and reapply a fresh layer of my new lip gloss. Then I actually take a few minutes to primp a little. For some reason it feels important to look extra feminine tonight. I even consider putting on that new bra that's still in the pink Victoria's Secret bag, but now I hear my mom calling me.

I grab my letterman jacket from the hook on the back of my door, then step out of my room and look down to the family room where Mom is standing. "What?"

"Is Jess picking you up for youth group tonight?" she asks with this curious and hopeful smile. Like she's thinking that whatever happened today will just miraculously blow over. Like I'm just going to forget that Jess has this warped fondness for chicks and move on. Yeah, right.

"Nope." I slip into my jacket. "BJ's giving me a ride tonight."

Mom places her hands on her hips and frowns up at me. "What about Jess?"

"What *about* Jess?" I turn away from her and go to my room to get my purse. But as I go down the stairs, she's still standing there, giving me that look.

"You're not just deserting her, are you, Ramie?"

I sling the strap of my purse over my shoulder and lock eyes with my mom. "Who deserted who?"

"Jess is in a tough place right now. Aren't you at least a little concerned about her?"

"Of course I'm concerned. I think she's lost her freaking mind. Why wouldn't that concern me?"

"But you're just going to cut her off? Quit being her friend simply because she told you that she's gay?"

I kind of shrug, then glance at the clock above the fireplace. "BJ should be here by now," I say quickly. "I'm going outside to meet her."

Mom just shakes her head as I walk past her. I can tell she is judging me, that she thinks I'm totally selfish, not to mention a worthless kind of friend. But then again my mom is not a Christian. She doesn't understand that the Bible draws clear lines between right and wrong, good and evil, gay and straight. My mom doesn't even believe in absolutes. How can she possibly get me?

"So what's up?" BJ asks as I get into her almost brand-new VW Bug. I still can't believe her parents got her this for her sixteenth birthday last summer. But then they've got money, and they probably think it's no big deal. And, as BJ told her friends, they also promised to take it away from her if her grades don't stay up. Not that they need to be worried. BJ's GPA is close to perfect and everyone is pretty sure she'll end up being valedictorian. Still, I can't help but feel a twinge of envy as I smell that new car smell and eye the little bud vase where she keeps a fake daisy. I mean she's only sixteen and I just turned seventeen in October and I still don't have a car. Not even an *old* one!

"Have you talked to Jess?" I venture as she pulls into traffic.

"Like since when?"

"You know, like *today*."

"No, I haven't seen her since basketball practice yesterday. By the way, you were looking really good out there, Ramie. I heard Coach Ackley telling Mrs. Cole that we might have a chance at state if you keep playing like that once the season starts."

I kind of shrug. "That's cool."

"So what's the deal with Jess? Why didn't you ride with her tonight? Not that I mind giving you a ride. But is she sick or something? I mean she seemed perfectly fine at practice. In fact, her game was looking pretty good too."

I'm not sure how much to say. I mean it's one thing for Jess to confide in me. I am, or rather I was, her best friend. But I'm just not sure whether I have the right to tell anyone else. "She's not sick," I tell BJ. "Well, not physically anyway."

"What do you mean? Is she going mental on us or something? Did she have some kind of meltdown?"

"Sort of." I let out a big sigh. "But I think she should tell you herself, BJ. I mean she only told me today, and it was kind of shocking, but I don't know if it's okay for me to tell anyone yet."

"Man, now you really got me curious. Now that I think about it, she has been kind of quiet lately. But she's been at every practice and she plays good and hard, so I'm thinking it's not like she's doing drugs or anything. Is she?" BJ looks worried.

I kind of laugh. "No, she's definitely not doing drugs."

"But she's not coming to youth group. Has she fallen away from the Lord or something?"

"I . . . I'm not really sure. You'll have to ask her that yourself."

"So, she *might* be there tonight?"

"Maybe. I don't really know."

"Did you guys have a fight?"

"No, not exactly. But her, uh, her little announcement has put kind of a damper on our friendship."

"Ah-hah!" BJ sounds excited now, like she might've stumbled onto the right answer. "Do you two like the same guy?"

"No, no," I say quickly.

"Are you sure? I mean I noticed that you've kind of had your eye on Mitch Bryant lately. Do you think that Jess is—"

"No," I insist. "It's nothing like that. But what're you talking about? How did you know I like Mitch? I mean not that I do."

She laughs. "Yeah, right. Hey, I'm not stupid, Ramie. I saw you talking to him during practice last week. You seemed pretty tuned in to every word he was saying and he was eyeing you like he—"

"Hey, he was just being nice. He came by to help the coach with that new laptop that's been driving him nuts. Then Mitch gave me a little shooting pointer," I tell her, which isn't completely untrue. "And it actually worked. Remember, he used to be pretty good, back in middle school anyway."

"Well, you could clean his clock now, Ramie."

I laugh. "Yeah, right."

To my relief, we talk about basketball and my possibilities with Mitch during the rest of the short drive to church.

"Do you think Mitch will be here tonight?" BJ asks as we walk toward the lit-up youth building.

"I wouldn't have the slightest clue," I tell her. And that's the truth. I mean, despite the fact that Mitch's dad is the senior pastor here (a fact I still can't completely wrap my mind around), Mitch has been pretty random when it comes to going to youth group or camps or anything. I mean, I'm sure he must be a Christian and everything. But he's just never been that into the youth activities.

When we get inside the building, I'm pleasantly surprised to see that Mitch is actually here. He's leaning against the doorframe and talking to Nathan Gallagher, our youth pastor.

"Hey, Ramie," Mitch says to me as we pause by the door. "Hey, BJ. What's up?"

I smile at him. "Not much."

"These girls have been looking really hot out there on the basketball court lately," he says to Nathan.

"Basketball?" asks Nathan with interest.

"Yeah," says BJ. "Games don't start until after Christmas."

"And I thought you were just into volleyball and soccer, Ramie."

"It's a way to keep in shape," I tell him.

"Well, she's doing way more than that," says Mitch. "The girls' varsity team has some real potential."

I shrug. "We're okay."

Then Mitch gives me a playful punch in the arm. "Ramie's too humble. You should see her. She's a star."

I roll my eyes at him. "I'm okay." I nod toward BJ. "But you should see this girl on defense. Our team wouldn't have a chance if she didn't get in there and steal the ball the way she does."

"And Jess is a force to be reckoned with too," adds BJ.

"Hey, where *is* our Jess tonight?" asks Nathan, glancing over our shoulders like he expects her to pop in right behind us. Of course, this sends a chill down my spine. Really, the last person I want to see right now is Jessica LeCroix. And if it wasn't wrong (and I'm not even totally sure that it *is* wrong), I would pray to God right now; I would beg him to keep Jess away. At least for tonight. I'm just not ready to see her again. Not yet. *Please, God! Have mercy.*

"I'm not sure where she is," I say.

Then we chat a little more about the future of Greenville High's girls' varsity basketball team.

"Women's sports have come a long way since I was in high school," admits Nathan. "Of course, that was back in the dark ages."

We all laugh, but I'm reminded that despite Nathan's hip haircut and sideburns, he's almost as old as my mom.

"But they actually take you girls seriously now," he continues. "Back in my day, girls' sports were more for losers."

BJ laughs. "Well, they still don't take us as seriously as they do the guys' sports. They still get top billing, better uniforms, and the best game schedules."

"But that's just because of the old bottom line," I add. "Their games are the ones that bring in the big bucks."

Mitch winks at me. "Well, I'll be coming to the women's basketball games. You can count on that."

I smile at him. And then I wonder about what BJ said earlier tonight. Is it possible that Mitch might really be into me? And, if so, wouldn't that be the perfect escape from this dilemma with Jess and her questionable sexual orientation? Plus, it would be the perfect way to show people that I'm not like her, that just because I was once her best friend doesn't mean I'm a lesbian too. I can feel the heat on my face just thinking this. Just the idea that this skanky news will be out in the open soon, at least I assume it will, makes me feel sick all over again.

I try to push these disturbing thoughts away from my mind as the music starts up. We have the coolest band to lead worship. I can really get into the clapping and the songs and everything. And before I know it, Jessica LeCroix is the furthest thing from my mind. And from my heart.

But when Nathan shares about how God wants us to *love our enemies*, the only enemy I can think of is Jess. And I have absolutely no desire to love her. All I want to do is to forget her — to forget that I ever knew her. Okay, I finally do feel some conviction coming on. It starts when Nathan explains how we should *pray* for our enemies. I guess I can do that.

I can pray that God will show her that being gay is wrong, that it is sin against our Creator. I can pray that God will convict her heart and that she will rethink this whole crazy thing. I can pray that Jess will realize that she really isn't a lesbian, and that she doesn't even want to be. And I can pray that she will call me up tonight and that she will say that she was totally wrong and that she is terribly sorry. And that she's taking it all back.

Hopefully she will take it all back before anyone, besides me and my mom, finds out.

five

I USUALLY RIDE TO CHURCH WITH JESS ON SUNDAY MORNINGS. BUT I'M NOT terribly surprised when she doesn't call or come by to get me. Mostly I'm relieved. I didn't even bother to get dressed. I figured if by some weird chance she did show up, she would see that I was still in my pajamas, and I could pretend not to feel well. Of course, she would get my hidden meaning. But that seems the easiest route for the time being. No need to beat her over the head with how upsetting this behavior of hers is. At least not yet. I'm not sure how long I'll be able to keep my mouth shut. Surely, she must realize that I will have an opinion.

By eleven I feel pretty certain that I won't be seeing her today. Big sigh. Although I'm still curious as to whether she went to church today. I'm sure her parents would go, since they rarely miss a service. And I imagine her older sister, Kaye, and Kaye's husband and baby would be there. At least I guess they'd be there. But what if they already know about Jess's big disclosure? What if they, like me, feel embarrassed and uncomfortable about this? What if they don't want to be seen with her? Who can blame them?

I think people who decide to become gay should consider these things more carefully, especially before they jump out of the closet and scare everyone to death. They should think about how their new "orientation" completely disorients others around them. They should consider the unfairness of their selfish and sinful choice, and how it hurts all the people who love and care about them. Like Jess's older brother Alex. He's in seminary right now, and he and Jess have always been close. She's always looked up to him. And he was always so supportive of her. More than anyone else in her family, he encouraged her love of sports. What will Alex think of her now?

"You didn't go to church," Mom brilliantly observes as she comes into the living room with her newspaper and a cup of coffee.

"No, I didn't."

"Still stewing over Jess?"

I shrug. "I just felt like sleeping in."

Her brows give that little lift that's meant to say she doesn't believe me. But she just sips her coffee and opens her paper.

Relieved that she doesn't plan to "practice" any counseling techniques on me right now, which I think is considered unethical and maybe even illegal, I get up and go to my room, where I pop in a CD and flop down on my bed. I need to think. Really, what am I going to do about this? Is there anything I can do? I mean besides pray? I've been begging and begging God, asking him to do something to undo the mess Jess has made. And so that's what I decide to do now. I will continue asking God to reveal to Jess that she's made a big mistake. I ask him to show her that she's really not gay, and she doesn't want to be gay, and that homosexuality is a sin.

I keep on praying like this until I hear a knock at my door, which makes me jump, and I almost expect Jess to walk in. What would I do then?

"Hey, Ramie," calls my mom. "I'm going to the fitness club with Brenda now. Do you want to come?"

"No thanks," I call back.

"We might grab a bite to eat afterward," she says.

I laugh. "Well, as long as you're not going for pizza or cheese-burgers," I warn her. "That might void your workout."

"Yeah, yeah. See you later."

I feel a little guilty for not going, since I was the one to talk Mom into joining the fitness club in the first place. To encourage her, I joined too. We got a great two-for-one deal, and during summer I used to go with her at least three times a week. But then her friend Brenda stepped in and joined the club, and since I get more than enough exercise with my sports during the school year, I have stepped out. My mom has had a weight problem since I can remember. She's always going on some kind of diet, but then she cheats and ends up being even heavier than before. But the fitness club seems to be working. And it's nice to see her shedding a few pounds. I know it makes her happier too. I'm glad to see she's sticking with it.

Even so, the house feels really empty after Mom leaves, and it occurs to me that I don't usually spend this much time here on my own. I suppose some people might think I was moping, or maybe just avoiding something—or *someone*. Usually Jess and I hang out together after church on Sundays. Sometimes I go to her house or sometimes we go out and try to find something to do. But suddenly I feel kind of alone. Kind of lonely.

Our townhouse has three levels. The first level has the garage and the master bedroom, my mom's domain. The second level has a kitchen and family room that's fairly spacious, with lots of windows that overlook a nice view of the rolling hills. The third level is all mine. It has a smaller bedroom and bath. But because it's on the third level and my mom's not exactly in great shape yet, she hardly ever comes up here. Consequently, it can get pretty messy. I blame this on my busy extracurricular schedule.

I mean, we just barely finished volleyball season, which happens to be my favorite sport. The state tournament was like, two weeks ago. I was disappointed that we only took third, but then some of our stronger players graduated last year. Anyway, I had all of four days to recover from volleyball and suddenly it's basketball season. The truth is, I didn't really want to play basketball. But Jess talked me into it. At the time I told myself that it would be a good way to stay in shape for spring soccer, my second favorite sport, and I can hold my own on the basketball court besides. But now I'm starting to wonder.

So I blame my packed schedule for the condition of the third floor, and if Mom ever came up here, I'm sure I could create a convincing defense. But since I have nothing better to do today, and I'm tired of thinking about *stuff*, I decide to roll up my sleeves and clean up my space. As I work, I tell myself that maybe God is watching me. Maybe he'll be pleased with my obedience (because Mom really does expect me to keep this part of the house clean), and he'll honor me by answering my prayers in regard to Jess. Anyway, it seems a good theory as I crank up my CD player and turn this cleaning routine into an aerobic workout.

Finally, it's almost five o'clock. I've just hauled the last basket of clean laundry back upstairs and am putting the still warm-from-the-dryer sheets on my bed when I hear my cell phone ringing from inside my purse. But I don't want to answer it, since Jess is about the only one who ever calls me on my cell phone. Well, besides my mom, that is. And if it is Jess, which I'm sure is the case, I don't want to talk. Just the same, I grab the phone and check the caller ID, but it's a number I don't recognize. So I decide to risk it.

"Hello?"

"Hey, Ramie," says a guy's voice. "This is Mitch."

"Hey, Mitch," I reply as I fall backward onto my half-made bed with huge, enormous relief, not to mention a bunch of curiosity. "What's up?"

"I got your cell phone number from the youth-group directory at church," he tells me. "Hope you don't mind."

I laugh. "Not at all. It's not like I'm trying to stay unlisted or anything."

"Well, I was just thinking about you today and I wondered if you'd like to see a movie or something?"

I sit up straight now. Is this for real? Is Mitch really asking me out? Does he actually want to take *me* on a real date? No, I tell myself, it's probably just a friendly kind of thing. He's just being nice. Well, whatever!

"Yeah, sure," I tell him in a calm voice, trying to hold back my enthusiasm. No need to look too desperate. I mean it's not like I've never gone out with a guy before. Even if it was only once.

"Cool." Then he tells me the title of the movie, and it turns out to be something I actually wanted to see. "Pick you up a little before seven then?"

"Sounds good." I'm doing the mental math now. My curfew on school nights is ten, and I think I'm safe.

After I hang up, I do a happy dance! I turn up my music even louder and I totally get down in my nicely cleaned room. This is so cool! *So cool!* In some ways it almost makes up for this thing with Jess. Almost. Anyway, it will be a good distraction. Not just for me either, because I'm thinking that if by some miracle I can get Mitch seriously interested in me, as in dating regularly, well, maybe that will distract others from drawing any false conclusions about me and my *ex*–best friend. I can only hope.

When Mom gets home, I'll tell her the news. And here's one of the benefits of having a liberal type of mom. She'll be totally cool with it. She doesn't have problems with me dating. Well, as long as I don't get pregnant. Seriously, she's not even too opposed to premarital sex. I know this for a fact since she's given me her little sex talk enough times. "Just make sure that you always use protection," she's warned me more times than I care to recall. "And make sure that you save that first time for someone really special."

Of course, this just makes me laugh, and then I usually end up telling her something like, "Yeah, someone special—*like my husband on my wedding night!*" Of course, then she just gives me that patronizing smile of hers, like she knows everything about everything, and I am still so young and inexperienced. But I do plan to prove her wrong. Someday, she will be at my wedding, like ten or more years from now, and she will know that I remained a virgin, and she will know that I chose to wait, to save myself, and she will see that my husband is so glad that I did, and that God is going to bless our marriage . . .

"Ramie," calls my mom from downstairs.

I go and stick my head out over the landing. "Did you have a good workout?" I ask in pleasant voice.

She tosses me a slightly guilty smile. "Yes, we did. Although we probably overindulged afterward." Then she confesses to getting the big-size sandwich at Schlotzky's. "And chips! But I brought you a pastrami on rye," she says, holding up a red-and-green bag.

"Sounds good," I tell her. "I've been cleaning my room all day and I'm starving!"

"Wow." She looks impressed. "Good for you, Ramie."

"And I'm going to the movies with Mitch Bryant tonight. He'll be here in about half an hour," I say as I run down the stairs to retrieve the food.

She nods. "Have I met Mitch before?"

I kind of laugh. Like has Mom met any guys that I know before? The only place where Mom ever meets my friends is at my games, which doesn't happen all that often, since she doesn't come to that many anymore. And then the friends she meets are usually girls.

"No, Mom," I tell her as she gives me the bag. "You haven't met him. But I've known him for years. His dad is the senior pastor at our church. Remember? You've heard me mention Pastor Bryant, haven't you?"

"Yes, that sounds familiar." Then she gets this funny look. "Dating a pastor's son, Ramie? Are you sure about this?"

"Why not?" I feel defensive now. Why is she always in attack mode when it comes to anything that has to do with my church or being a Christian?

"Haven't you ever heard about PKs?" she asks with a sly grin.

"PKs?"

"Preachers' kids." She winks at me. "They're usually the wildest of the bunch."

"Oh." I roll my eyes at her. "Well, not Mitch. He's just a regular guy, Mom. Don't worry. He's not wild."

"Just remember what I've told you, Ramie," she begins. "If you get into a situation where—"

"Yeah, yeah," I say, waving my hand to shut her up before she embarrasses both of us again. Then I head back up the stairs. "Trust me, Mom," I yell over my shoulder. "I remember! Not that I need to remember! Thank you very much!"

Later on, when I'm actually out with Mitch, and he's driving toward the city in this very cool 1966 Mustang that he and his dad restored, I am doing everything I can to keep my mom's crazy warning about PKs, combined with her old familiar "protection lecture," from running rampant through my mind. Why does she do that to me? It's like telling someone not to think about pink elephants! *Sheesh!*

"You seem pretty quiet tonight," Mitch says as he turns in at the theater complex. "Something bothering you?"

"No," I say quickly. But then I rethink this. Why not be honest with him? Well, at least partially honest. Of course, I won't tell him everything about my life on our first date. And I certainly don't plan on telling him about Jess. "Actually, I was obsessing about my mom." I laugh. "She can be pretty weird sometimes." Then I tell him a little about her, how she's a family counselor and pretty liberal. "She's also sort of antichurch," I finally say, thinking I should just get these minor cards out on the table.

He laughs. "I think she sounds pretty cool."

"Well, she's nothing like your parents," I say. "I happen to think they're pretty cool."

"Maybe it's just that grass-is-greener kind of thing."

We're still joking about our parents as we go into the theater, and I'm thinking this is not going too bad. Then, before I have a chance to question whether this is really a date—like, am I supposed to buy my own movie ticket?—Mitch has already taken care of it.

"Wanna share a popcorn?" he asks.

"Sounds good."

"What do you want to drink?"

Turns out we both like Sierra Mist, so we decide to share the jumbo size, and I'm thinking, yeah, this *is* a date! Woo-hoo!

But then I see this older dude, who's waiting in the concessions line and just staring at us with this weird expression, and I wonder what's up with him? And then it hits me. Oh, yeah, he's bugged that Mitch, this blue-eyed blond guy, is out with this African American chick. And, naturally, that irritates me! Like, whose business is it anyway? And then the other part of this bugs me too, like why is it that although I am actually "half" Caucasian, I am still considered "black" in some people's narrow-minded eyes? I want to tell off this geezer, to tell him to get over it and to get a life, but I know that would only make things worse and it might embarrass Mitch. Instead, I just toss the jerk a great big smile. Since I was little, I've been told that I have a "winning" smile. I used to think the label referred to sports, because I do like to win. But then I read somewhere that it meant more like you could win people over with it. And to my surprise, the old geezer actually smiles back. Well, go figure!

The movie turns out to be great. And I can tell by the way Mitch is treating me, and how we joke as we share our popcorn and drink, that this really is a date. And I'm pretty sure that he is into me. And it's so amazing!

Unfortunately, it's nine forty when we get out of the theater. "Wow, that was a pretty long flick," I tell him as I look at my watch. "We'll just barely make it home by my curfew."

"Ten on school nights?" he asks, like he's reading my mind.

"Yeah. Unless I have an away game. That's an exception."

"Same here."

"So our parents agree on at least one thing." I laugh. "But that's probably where it ends."

We make some more jokes at our parents' expense, and then Mitch is pulling up to where I live. I'm halfway out of the car, not really sure what to do next, when I notice that Mitch is already out too, standing by the passenger door and offering me his hand. "Gotta walk you to the door," he says. "My dad taught me that one."

"So, what did your parents think about you taking me out?" I ask him as we walk toward my house. I've actually been wanting to ask him this question ever since the geezer gave us the eye at the theater, but up until now I just couldn't get up the nerve.

"They both like you, Ramie. They were totally cool with me asking you out."

I let out a little sigh of relief as we go up the stairs to the front door that opens onto the second floor. "Cool."

"So . . ." He reaches for my other hand now. "Can I kiss you good night? Or are you one of those girls who doesn't kiss on the first date?"

I consider this. I mean, on the one hand, I don't want to seem too easy. On the other, I don't want him to think I don't like him. And I really want to have another date with him.

"I guess one little kiss would be okay," I tell him. But even as I say this, I am starting to feel nervous. I mean I've only been kissed twice before. And the first time was at this totally lame middle-school party, where everyone was kissing pretty much everyone, and it probably shouldn't even count. The second time was that unfortunate first date that I keep trying to forget. But consequently, I'm not too sure that I'm a very good kisser. And besides that, I haven't even had a breath mint or anything.

But Mitch leans forward and I close my eyes and hold my breath and to my relief, it goes fairly smoothly. In fact, it goes rather nicely, and I'm thinking that maybe Mitch is more experienced at this than I am.

"Thanks for a fun night," I say, surprised at how breathless my voice sounds. But maybe it's the cold November air.

"Thank *you!*" He grins at me like he's really happy. "I had fun too. Let's do it again sometime."

"Cool!" Then I turn and go into the house. I've barely closed and locked the front door before I fish my cell phone out of my purse and start to push Jess's speed-dial number. But then I stop. I can't believe it! I was about to call Jess! What was I thinking? Of course, it's understandable that my first impulse after an incredible night like this would be to call my best friend. She's always the one I call when something big happens. And this is huge! But then I tell myself, everything's changed. Like that was then and this is now, and Jessica LeCroix is no longer my best friend. Like a slap in the face or a firm shake, I firmly remind myself that *Jess is a lesbian.*

But as I slowly walk up the stairs to my room, I feel this hard lump growing in my throat. And for the first time since she told me her shocking "news" I am beginning to feel sad. Really, really sad. I feel like I'm grieving over the death of a loved one. Like I've just heard that my old best friend, the one I should be talking to right now, was suddenly killed in an explosion.

"Is that you, Ramie?" Mom calls from her bedroom downstairs.

"Yeah, Mom," I call back. "I'm home."

"Did you have fun?"

"Yeah, it was great. Night, Mom."

"Good night, Ramie."

Then I go into my room and I shut the door and I cry.

six

FORTUNATELY FOR ME, MY MOM DOESN'T HAVE ANY EARLY COUNSELING appointments Monday morning, and I am able to bum a ride to school from her. It hadn't even occurred to me yesterday that losing my best friend also meant losing my ride to school.

"Sorry I can't pick you up after practice," Mom tells me as she backs out of the garage. "I have a group therapy session that won't finish until eight."

I let out a groan. "Guess I get to ride home on the delightful activities bus."

"Oh, Ramie." Mom just shakes her head. "You're going to have to get over your homophobia, you know."

"Homophobia?" I shoot back at her. "That's totally nuts, Mom. It's not like I'm afraid of Jess, you know. I just don't happen to agree with her choice to sin like this. And I don't want to be around her. That is *not* homophobia!"

She makes a little noise that sounds kind of like *tsk tsk*, but I pretend to ignore her. Instead I hit her with my old begging routine, telling her again just how badly I really need a car.

"All my friends have cars," I say as we get closer to school.

"Then ask all your friends for rides."

"Mom," I plead. "If I had my own car, I could help you

more. I know how tired you are after work. I could do things like get groceries or pick up your dry cleaning or run errands or anything."

"I've already told you that our budget is tight, Ramie. If you really want a car, you'll have to get a job and help out with it."

"But I have sports."

"I know. And I think that's great, honey. It's just that we all have to make our choices. Personally, I think participating in sports is the right choice for you." She turns and smiles at me. "You're so good at them."

"So, because I'm good at them, I don't get a car," I complain. "Great little payoff."

"Having a car would mean car payments, insurance payments, gas money, repair costs . . ." She shakes her head. "Look, Ramie, if money was no object, I'd love to give you a car. I'd do it in a heart-beat. But right now we can't afford it."

We're almost at school now, and I can tell I've lost this argu-ment. Big surprise there. But I decide to pout just a little longer. No harm in letting her feel my pain, as she likes to put it.

"Cheer up," she tells me. "And maybe not having a car will help you to get over this thing with Jess a little faster. Who knows? Maybe by the end of the day she'll be giving you a ride home and everything will be back to normal."

"And maybe she'll kiss me good-bye after she drops me off," I say as Mom pulls up to the curb. "And maybe she'll ask me to be her date for the Winter Dance, and maybe we'll get married and I'll have artificial insemination and you can have lots of gay grandkids at Christmastime!"

"Oh, Ramie!" She looks exasperated now.

But I just give her an innocent look. "Does that bother you,

Mom? I figured the idea of Jess and me living happily ever after was just what you wanted."

"Have a good day, dear."

"Yeah, right!" Then I close the door just a little too firmly as I can see the frown across her brow, and I wonder why I'm treating her like this. It's not like this is her fault. And, more disturbing than that, I know that God would not be pleased by my little hissy fit or my disrespectful attitude. So I say a quick "I'm sorry" prayer as I slowly walk toward the school. What is wrong with me?

As I walk through the doors and security, I am filled with apprehension. I mean who knows what lies ahead today? It's quite possible that Jess has told others by now. Everyone in the school might be whispering about her, laughing behind her back or maybe to her face. And they could be laughing at me too. Oh, I so do *not* want to see her today!

Of course, I realize this is unlikely since we have three classes together. And then there's basketball practice after school. Maybe I should've been sick today. But, no, I tell myself as I walk toward the locker bay. That might've put me at a disadvantage in this little game. As I get closer to our row of lockers it occurs to me that it's not only my locker, it is also Jess's. It's like I almost forgot that we share a locker! Dear God, please help me.

I'm tempted to skip going to my locker altogether, but I really need to get my geometry book. And so when I come to the row where our locker is located, feeling like a foreign spy, I "accidentally" drop a pencil. I bend down to pick it up, glance down the row and see, to my relief, Jess is not there. Then I hurry to my locker and after blowing the combination twice, which I never do, I finally get the stupid thing open, retrieve the geometry book as well as my French book, which I really don't need until after lunch, and I shove them both into my backpack. I make a mental note to stop by the counseling center and demand that I get a different locker. Even if I have to explain the circumstances. Surely, they would understand.

By fourth period, it has become obvious that Jess is just as uncomfortable seeing me as I am seeing her. It's like we've signed a mutual avoidance pact, which suits me just fine. Still, I can tell that others are noticing. I mean it's not like Jess and I have a ton of friends. But we do have some. Mostly from church and sports and just life, I guess. By lunchtime, some of them are starting to ask questions. And, to my relief, Jess is making herself pretty scarce.

"You guys didn't get into a fight, did you?" says BJ in a slightly accusing tone.

"Huh?" I try out my innocent routine as I struggle to tear open a packet of dressing and then slowly squeeze it onto my chef's salad.

"Remember?" she persists. "I asked on Saturday night if you guys were having a fight, and you said no."

"We're *not* having a fight."

"Then why is Jess acting so weird?" asks Amy Temple. Amy, like Jess, is really into softball. They play both spring and summer leagues. And usually Amy and Jess get along great, although I'm not sure what Amy will think when she finds out about this. Amy already has a tough time with the women's softball coach, since she's pretty sure that Coach Reeves is gay, although no one knows this for sure. Still, we all agree that the woman is pretty butch both in appearance and behavior, and we all try to keep a safe distance from her. At least I thought we did. Now I'm not so sure about Jess.

"Yeah, Ramie," says BJ. "Why is she acting so weird?"

"Don't ask me," I say as I stab my fork into a piece of hard-boiled egg.

"Well, you can't ask Jess," says Amy. "She's not talking to anybody."

I peer at Amy. "Really? She's not talking to you either?"

"She's not talking to *anyone*," says BJ.

I glance over at Lauren, another sports friend. "How about you?"

"Nope."

"What do you mean exactly?" I question them. "Are you saying that you can say something to Jess and that she completely ignores you?"

"Not exactly," admits Amy. "It's more like she just blows you off."

"Yeah, she just gives a snippy answer, then looks away like she's too busy, like she doesn't have time for you."

"Like she hates us all."

"Did we do something to offend her?" asks Lauren.

I roll my eyes and let out a big sigh.

"You do know something, don't you, Ramie?" Amy points her unopened straw at me.

"She does," confirms BJ. "She admitted as much to me on Saturday night. But you also said that Jess would tell me herself, Ramie. But she hasn't. So what's up with that?"

"Yeah, Ramie, spill the beans," says Lauren.

"Come on," urges Amy. "If Jess is having some kind of problem, you should tell us. We're her friends. Maybe we can help her."

Now I'm not sure what to do. I remember what Mom told me, how Jess really needs her friends right now. And it does occur to me that telling these guys could take some of the pressure off me. Kind of like they'd suddenly be involved in this sticky dilemma too. On the other hand, it might really hurt Jess if I let this out. And, as mad as I am at her, I guess I'm starting to feel a tiny bit sorry for her too. I mean, how can she be so set on ruining her life? Who does that?

"It's complicated," I tell my friends. "And I really think you should hear it from her. Okay?"

Lauren's eyes light up now. "I know!" She says, pointing her spoon into the air. "I know what it is!" Then she gets this slightly appalled look on her face and sets her spoon back into her bowl of half-eaten chili with a dull clunk.

"What?" demands BJ. "What is it, Lauren?"

"Nothing." Lauren doesn't look up. And I think maybe she really does know. But how? How could she have figured this out? Or is it possible that she's involved too? The mere idea of this is so disturbing that I want to shove it away from me. How messed up would it be if Jess wasn't the only one? I study Lauren for a moment and realize that she does have kind of a strong masculine side. Not that it means she's gay. But I suppose it means she *could* be.

"Come on," Amy pleads with her. "You gotta tell us now, Lauren. You can't say you know and then keep it to yourself. Out with it!"

Lauren just slowly shakes her head. She keeps staring down at her soup, looking like she really is about to be sick.

"Lauren," I say to her in an urgent tone, and she looks up at me with worried eyes. "Do you *really* know?"

"Not really."

"Come here." I stand and pull on her arm. "Come tell me what you think without anyone else listening."

"Oh, man," says BJ. "Talk about middle school."

"Yeah," chimes in Amy, "like a déjà vu all over again."

But I ignore them as I practically drag Lauren off to a quiet corner of the cafeteria. "Tell me what it is that you think you know, Lauren," I command her.

I can see her swallow hard, and I know she doesn't want to say the words out loud. Who does?

"Come on, Lauren. I'll tell you whether or not you're right, okay? Because I do know what's up with Jess."

"Okay." She looks to her left and to her right and then over her shoulder before she asks in a quiet voice, "Is Jess gay?"

I blink, then nod. "But how did you know?" Of course what I really want to ask her is, *Are you gay too?* Because that might explain her suspicion about Jess and why she knows. Still, I know that would be pretty intrusive, not to mention stupid. And I suspect that I've already pushed her too hard, because she actually seems even more upset now that I've confirmed this is true. Seriously, I don't want the poor girl falling apart on me right here in the cafeteria. Still, I'm curious. "Really, Lauren, how did you find out about Jess?"

"Last week," she begins in a hushed tone. "I can't remember what day it was, but early in the week . . . it was after school and I was on my way to practice when I saw Jess going into the counseling center. She didn't see me, so I started to yell at her, but before I did, she ducked into the conference room in there."

"So?"

"Well, remember those colorful posters that were plastered all over the school, the ones about the gay alliance and their sexual-orientation meeting? There'd even been an announcement about it during—"

"That's right! That meeting was supposed to be on *Tuesday in the conference room in the counseling center*, and I remember some of us were making fun of it during English when the announcement came on. I actually teased Joey Pinckney. I told him he should go to the meeting and see if he could find himself a boyfriend." Suddenly I feel really bad for teasing him like that. I remember the look on his face and how quiet he got. But I was just kidding. Everyone acts like that sometimes. It's just the way high school kids are. People really shouldn't get offended so easily. Still, maybe I should apologize. Both to him and Jess.

"That's weird." Lauren gets this funny look on her face.

"What?"

"I saw Joey that day too. I mean I can't say for sure that I saw him go into that room, but now that you mention it, I do remember seeing him hanging out in the counseling center. I thought it was kinda strange, but then Joey is kinda strange."

"Do you think he's gay too?"

She shrugs. "Guess it's not really our business. Besides, it's Jess who concerns me right now."

"Well, you're probably right about her going to that meeting. She'd told me earlier that day that she was going to miss practice because she had to do a chemistry lab, which I remember thinking was odd since I hadn't had any extra assignments in my chem class. But I'm sure that was just her cover-up so she could attend that meeting."

"I didn't really know what to think," admits Lauren, "but I decided not to mention it to anyone. Even when Jess missed practice, I sort of just told myself not to start imagining things."

"So now you know you weren't."

"Just because she went to that meeting . . ." Lauren looks uncertain. "I mean it doesn't prove anything. Going to a meeting doesn't make you a homosexual."

I kind of shrug, wishing we'd never had this conversation.

"But you said she was," Lauren persists.

"No, you *guessed* that she was."

Now Lauren looks at me with what seems a pretty suspicious

expression. I can almost tell that she's trying to put two and two together, and I know I need to stop her before she adds it up to equal *gay*.

"If it makes you feel any better, I was totally shocked by the news too," I say quickly. "Actually, Jess outed herself to me on Saturday. We were at the Greenville Mall when she told me. I swear I almost had a nervous breakdown."

"Seriously?" Lauren looks properly stunned now. "She told you that while you were at the mall? How does someone do that anyway? Were you guys like shoe shopping in Nordie's and she just turns to you and announces, 'I'm gay and what do ya think of these new Nikes?'"

"Not exactly," I admit. "I guess she did try to break it to me gently." I kind of laugh now. "Not that there's a way to break something like that gently." Then I go on to tell Lauren about how my lip actually went numb and how I had a meltdown in the restroom. "It was pretty weird."

"Wow."

"I just didn't think I should tell anyone," I continue. "I mean it's Jess's business. If she really wants to come out of the closet, well, don't you think it's up to her to let her friends know?"

"I guess."

"So, maybe we should just keep it to ourselves."

Lauren is looking over my shoulder now, back over to where we abandoned our lunches and our friends. "You really think they won't figure this out, Ramie?"

"I don't know."

"Well, I'll do my best to keep my mouth shut. But this is going to be tough to hide. I mean Amy's already pretty homophobic anyway. You know how she runs whenever Coach Reeves gets too close."

"Don't we all."

"Apparently not *all* of us, Ramie."

"Yeah, whatever. Just the same, I really think we have to keep a lid on this, Lauren." I'm tempted to tell her about how I've been praying about this, how I've been hoping that God will get a hold of this thing and that he'll convict Jess of her sin before it's too late and everyone finds out. Still, I know that Lauren's not a Christian. And I doubt that she'll really get me. Instead I say something that sounds uncomfortably like my mom.

"You know, Jess is really going to need her friends' support on this. Some people will probably ostracize her. It shouldn't be us, Lauren. The kindest thing we can do is to wait for Jess to out herself. Don't you think?" Okay, I know I sound totally hypocritical—at least to myself—and the truth is, I want this whole thing to just go away. I'd like to lock Jess permanently in the closet.

She nods. "Yeah. You're right. You really are a good friend to her, Ramie. I'm not sure that I'd be so cool if Amy suddenly announced something like this. I mean people might assume that just because we're best friends, I'm gay too."

Of course, I will never admit to Lauren that I was actually questioning her sexual orientation only minutes ago. Although I'm pretty much convinced by her reaction that she is not, and has no interest in becoming, a lesbian. That is a huge relief. It would be really disturbing if more girls involved in team sports started popping out of the closet. I'm sure everyone would just naturally start to think that if you're a girl and if you're into athletics . . . well, I just don't want to go there.

seven

It wasn't easy to ignore BJ and Amy as they pestered Lauren and me with questions about Jess. But it did help that I was no longer alone in this thing. And for some reason it's consoling that Lauren seems almost as upset about it as I am.

"This thing with Jess is really going to make the rest of us look bad," she says quietly to me after we leave the cafeteria. She sadly shakes her head. "I totally hate being called a 'girl jock,' Ramie. It just gets to me. And now Jess goes and does this."

I don't answer her. But I do understand.

"Hey, Ramie," calls a guy. I turn to see Mitch coming from behind us. I'm so happy to see him and so glad that he's the one approaching me. But I manage to keep my cool. I give Lauren a glance and she just nods with wide-eyed approval. Kinda like *go girl*. So I do.

"How's it going?" I ask him. I'd been watching for him all morning and during lunch but never saw him.

"Okay. But now I'm starving."

"You missed lunch?"

"Yeah. I went to that military recruiting meeting at the counseling center."

"Really? Are you interested in the military?"

"Maybe. I mean it probably sounds kinda lame, but I've always dreamed of going to the Air Force Academy."

"Isn't it hard to get in?"

He nods and holds up some papers and pamphlets. "But according to the recruiter, I might have a chance."

"Good for you. But too bad you missed lunch."

He grins. "Not really. My day's over now anyway."

I make a face at him. "Oh, that's right. Mr. Lucky Senior. You're only going half days."

"But that might change," he points out. "If I want to get into the academy, I'll have to beef up my schedule after Christmas."

"Are you thinking about it?"

"Yeah. But it also means I'll have to give up my job."

"Where do you work?" I ask as we pause near the front entrance.

He makes a funny face. "Well, if I told you, I'd have to kill you."

I laugh. "So you're with the FBI?"

"Something like that."

"Seriously," I prod. "Where do you work, Mitch?"

"Top secret."

I make my face into a pout. "Why?"

"Just because."

"Oh," I say in a slightly accusing way. "You're ashamed of your job. I get it."

He shrugs. "Or maybe it's just top secret."

"Or maybe you're a male stripper."

This makes him really laugh. And then he leans over and gives me a little peck on the cheek. "That's what I like about you, Ramie. You're not one of those goody-goody Christian girls."

I smile at him. Actually, I'm not quite sure whether that was a compliment, but decide to take it as one.

"Have fun at school," he tells me.

"Have fun taking it all off," I shoot back, which makes him laugh even louder. But as I walk away, I do wonder. Where *does* he work? And why is he so ashamed of it? Surely he's not really a male stripper! His parents would throw a fit! Then I feel embarrassed for even seriously thinking like that. I'm sure it has to do with all this stuff about Jess. It's like my head keeps getting stuck in Skankyville.

I pray as I hurry to French class. I ask God to forgive me for having bad thoughts, and I ask God to keep working on Jess. At least she doesn't take French, which gives me a little break from trying to avoid her. I realize there is still health class, which we have together, and then basketball practice after school. Health, I can survive. But the idea of getting dressed down for practice with Jess in the same locker room is a little creepy now—not to mention how disturbing it will be to use the same shower room after practice!

Now this just totally weirds me out. I mean, seriously, if Jess really is a lesbian, wouldn't she get turned on by looking at the naked girls in the shower? Oh, it makes me so sick! It seriously makes me want to hurl! This is so wrong. So unfair. How am I supposed to deal with this? I wonder if Lauren has considered this yet.

After French, I keep my promise to myself by going to the counseling center, where I ask to see Ms. Fremont. In some ways I think this woman should be held responsible for this big mess. After all, that meeting was held in her office. Isn't that like some kind of endorsement from her that becoming a homosexual is okay?

"Did you have an appointment?" the receptionist asks me.

"No, but this is urgent," I tell her. "I really need to see Ms. Fremont. It'll only take a few minutes."

The receptionist calls Ms. Fremont, and amazingly, I am allowed to see her.

"I was hoping we'd get to chat, Ramie," she starts in after asking me to sit down in the chair across from her.

Now I'm not sure what this means, but I'm guessing it has to do with Jess. "Sorry to just barge in like that," I say. "But I really needed to—"

"Don't worry about it. And, slow down, I have plenty of time to talk with you, Ramie. I'm sure you have a lot on your mind."

"Actually, I do."

"I know this must be a hard time for you. For both you and Jessica."

I nod. So she does know why I'm here. Well, that's a relief.

"But this is a safe place, Ramie. Whatever you say here will remain here. Do you understand?"

"Yes. I appreciate that." Now I'm wondering if I should do more than just demand a new locker. Maybe this is my chance to tell her all my concerns about the locker room and taking showers and—

"I wish you had been able to come to the meeting too, Ramie. I think it would've helped you to see that you're not alone in this. But I do understand your hesitancy. I know that it can be very hard to, well, as they say, come out of the closet." She kind of laughs. "Really, we need some better terminology."

"Wait," I say quickly. "You mean me? You mean you think I'm coming out of the closet too?"

"Well, I realize you might not be ready to tell people just yet. But that's exactly why the meeting would've been good for you. One of the points made was that you can't push these things. Timing is really critical. Especially with teens. And, really, there's no rush, Ramie. Still, I'm sure that it—"

"No!" I say, standing up and holding out both my hands as if to stop her flow of words. "That's not it! I am not coming out of the closet!"

"I understand that, dear," she says. "That's what I'm saying. No need to get upset. I'm just trying to validate your—"

"You don't understand," I say. "I am not coming *out* of the closet because I have never been *in* the closet. I am not gay! I don't want to be gay! Can't you get it?"

Now she looks slightly shocked. "Oh, I'm sorry, Ramie. I just naturally assumed that because you and Jess are so close—I mean such good friends—that you—"

"We used to be good friends," I tell her. "But after Jess told me about her . . . her sexual orientation, well, I can't handle it. We're not friends anymore. In fact that's why I'm here. We've been sharing a locker and I just can't do that anymore. I need my space, you know. This isn't easy."

She nods and makes a little note on the pad in front of her. "That can be arranged."

"I'm not trying to be mean," I say, not sure why I feel the need to defend myself. "It's just that this is pretty hard to deal with, you know?"

She nods again. "I'm sorry, Ramie. I can understand how you must feel. And if you ever need to talk about—"

"That's okay," I say quickly, thinking all I want is to get away from this crazy woman. I can't believe how easily she jumped to that conclusion. "I mean my mom's a counselor too. And she's been giving me a lot of good advice. But right now I just need a separate locker. Okay?"

"Okay." She hands me the note she's written. "Just take this to Mrs. Commons at the front desk in the office, and she'll take care of it. I've also asked her to give you an excuse for being tardy to class."

"Thank you." I'm already standing and halfway out the door.

"And, really, if you need to talk—"

"Thank you," I say again as I go out the door. "I'll keep that in mind."

My hands are shaking as I go to the front desk. What does it mean if the school counselor assumed I am a lesbian just because Jess is a lesbian? Doesn't this prove that everyone else will think exactly the same thing?

Mrs. Commons gives me a new locker and combination as well as a note for French class. But as I walk down the deserted hallway, I get this feeling that life as I know it will be ending shortly. What am I going to do? I decide to take advantage of my late excuse to remove my things from my old locker and relocate them into the new one. At least no one will see me doing it. And, really, I tell myself, I'm sure that Jess will be grateful for this too. It makes it easier for everyone.

Somehow I make it through my afternoon classes. To my relief, health isn't too terrible, and Jess sits far in the back, close to the door. Still, we have basketball practice to endure. Oh, what am I going to do?

After I've made one last trip to my new locker to deposit some things that I don't need to take home, I am finally heading toward the gym. I know that I'm running late, and yet I'm walking very slowly. I so don't want to do this. Seriously, I feel like I'm heading for my own execution. Like it's just a matter of time and I'm going to die. Oh, I suppose I'm making this into a much bigger deal than it should be. But that weird encounter with Ms. Fremont has left me feeling pretty freaked. I hate that she just assumed I am like Jess. Still, why wouldn't she? Why wouldn't everyone? Furthermore, what if they're right? I mean it's not like I've ever had a real boyfriend. Not that I don't want one.

This thing with Mitch, if he's not a male stripper, is giving me hope.

I'm about halfway to the gym when it occurs to me that there may be some options here. Like we girls could insist that Jess must dress down and shower somewhere else, somewhere away from us. Or we could even put pressure on Jess to quit basketball altogether. Well, that seems pretty harsh, since she really does love basketball. Even more than I do. Then it occurs to me that I could quit basketball. And if I did quit basketball, I might be able to get a part-time job and talk Mom into letting me get a car. As much as I like basketball, it's not my favorite sport.

I know it won't be easy to explain my decision to Coach Ackley. He was so excited for me to play, and it was pretty cool when he put me on varsity last week. Still, it's my life. And, to be fair, it was Jess who talked me into going out this year. And part of my reasoning was so I could catch rides home with her instead of riding the stupid bus. And our first preseason game isn't for another week, so it's not like I'm ruining the year for them.

On and on I go until I've finally reached the gym. Instead of going into the locker room, where my friends are probably still getting dressed, I go directly into the gym, straight to where Coach Ackley is dumping out a bag of basketballs.

"Why aren't you dressed down, Grant?" he asks me as I approach. Coach always calls us girls by our last names. "Something wrong?"

"Sort of."

He frowns. "What's going on? Are you sick?"

"Not exactly."

"What then?" He glances at his watch, then looks over to the door to the girls' locker room.

"I'm quitting the team, Coach," I tell him in what I hope sounds like a firm tone.

"What?" he barks.

"I'm quitting."

"Why?" He's scowling now and I can tell he's getting mad.

"It's, uh, well, it's personal."

"What do you mean *personal?*" He narrows his eyes at me.

"It's kind of hard to explain, Coach. But I just think it's for the best."

"Whose best?"

"Well, mine. And maybe another player's too."

He just shakes his head but seems to soften some. "I think you're making a big mistake, Grant. You've got some great potential. I wouldn't have put you on varsity if I didn't think so."

"Thanks, Coach. I appreciate that."

"But you still wanna quit?"

"I don't exactly want to."

"Then don't!"

"I have to." Suddenly I feel close to tears, something that all coaches hate to see from any of their players. "It's just that I don't really have a choice." I can hear the girls starting to come out of the locker room now, dashing for loose balls, and they're beginning to shoot.

"Big mistake, Grant," he says again, then he turns his attention to the other girls, yelling out some directions, and I can tell that practice is going to be grueling today. And, fine, it's probably my fault. No, I tell myself as I head for a side door. It's Jess's fault.

I can see my friends watching me now, but I just keep walking. Lauren has a slightly stunned look on her face, like she knows something is up. BJ and Amy just look really curious. But it's Jess's face that really catches my eye. And it's her expression that is burnt into my memory as I exit the gym and head out to where I'm hoping those big ugly yellow buses are still waiting.

Those dark eyes of hers were filled with pure terror. I could tell that she suspected I was telling the coach about her, telling him that she's a lesbian and that she should be thrown off the team. Despite how angry I've been at her, I felt sorry for her just then. I could feel her fear, and it hurt.

But as I get onto bus #39, I push those feelings away. After all, it's not like I told the coach. Or anyone for that matter. And if anyone should be feeling bad right now, it's me. Not only have I quit the team, giving up a season when I could've been a star, I am now sitting on a smelly school bus and there is something sticky on this seat. But I console myself with a Bible verse. "Greater love has no one than this, that he lay down his life for his friends." And that's what I think I've done today. I've laid down my life for Jess. Even if she's not my friend anymore. I've laid down my life for her. Maybe that's what Nathan meant by loving your enemies. Although, to be completely honest, I don't feel any love for Jess right now. Even my pity seems to be fading as I imagine her and my friends happily practicing without me. Maybe she'll be glad. Maybe my absence will just make her look better.

eight

AFTER I GET HOME, WHICH TAKES WAY TOO LONG SINCE THE STUPID BUS STOPS
and starts about every other minute, I eat a bowl of ice cream, then
start going through the classified section of the newspaper, looking
for some kind of part-time job possibilities. I circle several at the
Greenville Mall, all of them part-time holiday help, and think that
at least it's a start.

It seems weird to be home like this, and I'm really not sure what
to do with myself, but I finally turn on the TV and flop down on the
couch and watch *Oprah*. It's something I haven't done since summer,
when I was so obsessed with her shows that I actually begged my
mom to get TiVo so that I could record them. Of course, Mom told
me to forget it. But I'm one of those people who, if asked what one
person they'd like to have dinner with, would probably choose
Oprah Winfrey. Oh, it's not like I tell my friends this, but I really
admire the woman. I love her positive attitude and can-do spirit.
And I think that she's a Christian, but I do have one problem with
her. I don't understand why she doesn't just get married. She seems
to love Stedman. And I'm sure they sleep together. So why can't she
just make an honest man out of him and get married? Oh, well.

Today, Oprah has her best friend, Gail, on and they are talking,
it figures, about friendships between women. But I decide to listen,

to pay attention so that the next time I make a best friend, if I ever do, I will be more careful. I will make sure that I don't connect with someone who has any sexual identity issues. I will choose a girl with a steady boyfriend, maybe a long history of steady boyfriends. Not that I'm in a hurry. If anything, I should focus my attention on getting more involved with Mitch.

They're showing some scenes of young girls who are best friends and, despite myself, this reminds me of when I first met Jess. If only I'd known then that it was going to end like this. Maybe I wouldn't have climbed onto the roof that day.

It was summer, and we'd just moved to Greenville from the university town where my mom had finally finished her master's in counseling. For my whole life, all I'd known was student-family housing, where we'd lived in this tiny apartment with lots of other families living in identical apartments all around us. Families came and went, along with a bunch of different friends for me, but Mom and I lived there until I was eight, and I guess I figured we'd always live there. But then she graduated and got a job at a counseling center in Greenville, and we moved into a little rental house on Cypress Street.

Back in student-family housing, everyone took turns watching us kids and I'd never really had a real babysitter before, but for some reason Mom got it into her head that I needed one now. So she hired Shelby to watch me. Shelby was fourteen and addicted to soap operas. So, to entertain myself, I would go outside and climb up a piece of lattice that took me right onto the flat roof of the carport. From there I could access the slanted roof of the house, where I would climb to the top, then straddle the peak and just sit like a queen, looking out over the neighborhood. When I got bored or too hot, I would simply slide down the slanted roof and land in an overgrown heap of ivy. Shelby never had a clue.

"What are you doing up there?" called a dark-haired girl from down below one day.

"Sitting," I called back down to her.

"Can I come up?" she asked.

"I don't know," I called back. "Can you?"

Before I knew it, she was up on the roof, straddling the peak just behind me. "This is cool," she said.

"Yep," I agreed. Then we talked for a while, and I learned that, like me, she was going into fourth grade too.

"Are you a different race?" she asked, pointing to one of my bronze-colored arms.

"No," I told her. "I'm actually from a different planet."

That just made her laugh, and she never did ask me about my skin color again. Oh, I suppose I eventually told her my family history, but I'm sure it was several years later. As it turned out, Jess's older sister observed us sitting on the roof one day and immediately informed Jess's mom, who immediately informed my mom. Shortly after that, the babysitter was dismissed and Mrs. LeCroix offered to help keep an eye on me until school started. "As long as you keep off of roofs," she warned me.

Maybe it's this memory, or maybe it's the photos and stories and music on *Oprah*, or maybe it's simply the fact that I'm no longer on the girls' varsity basketball team, but now I am crying. I turn off the TV, then go up to my room where I turn on my computer and go online. I decide to Google some information by typing in "help for friends of homosexuals" and the first website on the list is for this Christian organization called Exodus International. And I go to it and begin to skim, and it's like someone has just thrown me a lifesaver. I grab onto the rope and I read testimony after testimony of people who have been "delivered" from homosexuality. And suddenly I think maybe there really is hope. I add this website to my favorites list, then I go back and Google my question again.

Only this time I find a website that says exactly the opposite. It says things like "people are born this way" and that "they make good parents" and that "conversion therapies like those used by Exodus International seldom work and can be psychologically damaging." But, I remind myself, that was written by non-Christians. Of course they would say things like that. So would my mom.

Even so, I feel encouraged by the Christian site and suddenly I get an idea. I decide to e-mail what I've found to Jess. But then I'm not sure what to say. And so I simply write "check this out" in the subject box, and inside the e-mail I paste the website's domain address. Okay, I know that's not very personal, not to mention a cowardly way to share this information, but under the circumstances, I think it's best.

After that, I wander around my quiet house for about an hour, tormenting myself with lots and lots of questions. First of all, how many days can I stand to live like this? Why did I give up basketball? Why am I letting Jess control my life? How will I ever get a job, and even if I get a job, how will I get there? I know how Mom hates for me to use public transportation. What am I going to do? Is it possible that I'm going crazy? Finally I hear my cell phone ringing and dash up the stairs, wondering who it might be. And if it's Jess, will I be able to answer? To my huge relief it's Mitch (I know his number now), and he is calling from work.

"Having a slow night?" I tease. "Or do employment laws force the boss to give male strippers a break?"

He laughs. "Okay, Ramie, enough with the stripper jokes. I'm not a male stripper."

"Oh, good."

"Although I'm guessing they make better money than I do."

"What *do* you do?"

"Like I said, it's top secret."

"Come on, Mitch," I persist. "It's not really top secret, is it?"

"Well, it's *my* top secret."

"You mean nobody knows where you work?"

"Nobody but me and my boss and my parents."

"That is so weird."

"Yeah, I know."

"People shouldn't have secrets," I say, then instantly remember that I'm covering up one of the biggest secrets of my life.

"Maybe not, but they do." He pauses. "But I might be willing to exchange my secret if you tell me a secret about yourself."

I laugh. "This sounds like a setup."

"No, but it might come in handy for blackmail."

"You'd blackmail me?" I say in a wounded tone. "I thought we were friends."

"I thought we were more than friends," he says, and I feel a warm rush running through me.

"If we were more than friends, wouldn't you be willing to tell me where you work?" I ask.

"Maybe." Then he switches gears. "How was practice tonight?"

"Practice?" I say in a weak voice.

"Yeah, you know, dribbling the ball up and down the court, shooting baskets, practice. How was it? Are you still a superstar?"

This makes me feel kind of sick inside. Like, really, what was I thinking to give that up? To throw it all away? "Oh, Mitch," I say, choking back more tears.

"What's wrong, Ramie?"

"Me. Life. Everything."

"Seriously, Ramie, what's wrong? You sound really upset."

"I guess I am upset. Everything is such a mess."

"Are you home now?"

"Yeah."

"Well, I was just getting ready to leave. You want me to stop by? Do you need to talk?"

"Could you? I really do need to talk, Mitch. But I'm not sure if—"

"I'm on my way. You got anything to eat there?"

"I'll look around," I tell him. Then I hang up, dry my tears, put on some lip gloss and even brush my teeth. You never know. Then I go down to the kitchen in search of something to fix. It's just a little after six, and Mom won't be home for a while yet. Not that having Mitch here is a problem. I'm sure she wouldn't care one way or another. Finally, I decide on tomato soup and grilled-cheese sandwiches. I hope Mitch isn't picky.

"Smells good in here," he says as I let him inside.

"Thanks." Then I take his jacket and lead him into the kitchen.

"I like your house," he says as he looks at what I've concocted. "And that looks yummy!"

So we sit down at the island and eat and before long he is asking me what's wrong and why I was so upset.

I set my half-eaten sandwich back on my plate. I really don't feel very hungry anyway. Then I tell him I quit the team.

"You what?" He stares at me with a creased brow.

"I quit. Today."

"Why?"

"Why?" I echo. "This is where the story gets complicated," I tell him, looking down at my bowl of soup.

"I can handle complicated," he says as he dips his sandwich into his soup and takes a big bite. "Try me."

"I know," I say. "Let's make a deal. I'll tell you a secret, if you tell me where you work."

"Hey, is this a trick?"

I shake my head with a somber expression. "Trust me. My secret is pretty big. And I need some kind of reassurance that you won't tell anyone."

"You really quit the team?" he says again.

"Yeah. Coach Ackley was really ticked too."

"Can't blame him."

"Okay. That leads me to believe that you have a *real* secret, Ramie. And so I will tell you where I work if you also promise not to tell anyone else. *Deal?*" He sticks out his hand to shake now. And we lock eyes and shake. "All right, you also need to promise not to laugh. Okay?"

"Okay."

"I'm a computer geek."

"Huh?"

"You know those guys you see on the commercial, who wear the geeky outfits and drive those funny little cars and go help people to figure out their computer problems? That's my job. It's what I do. I'm a computer geek. And I really don't want anyone else to know about it. Okay?"

I smile. "Okay. And, actually, I think that would be a cool job. In fact, now that I quit the team, I'm thinking about getting a job myself. I thought I might start earning enough money to buy a car."

"Wait, wait," he says. "First I want to hear your big secret, Ramie. Then you can share all your future plans with me."

I take in a deep breath. "Okay. And I think it might feel good to get it out. It's like I'm starting to feel like I'm going crazy, you know.

The weird thing is that it's not really my secret. But it's something that someone told me. And, well, it's just pretty disturbing and — "

"Come on, Ramie. Just tell me."

"Jess is a lesbian."

He kind of blinks. "Really?"

I nod. "She told me last Saturday, which oddly enough seems like about a year ago. I went into shock when she told me. I mean, seriously, my lip went numb and then I actually threw up." For some reason I feel a need to make this clear to him. I do *not* want him making any assumptions like Ms. Fremont today.

"Man, that's gotta be tough, Ramie."

"It is. I mean, Jess used to be my best friend. And now, well, I can't stand to be around her. She makes me sick, Mitch. And that makes me feel even worse. I got my locker changed today. And then just the thought of being with her in the locker room, the shower room, well, it might sound stupid to a guy, but it was really nauseating."

"No, I know what you mean. I used to play baseball with this kid named Shane, and the guys all thought he was gay. And sometimes I'd see him looking at me, and it didn't make me sick, but it did make me mad. I wanted to go over and just take him down."

"Oh."

"But I didn't."

"That's good."

"So, I know what you mean, Ramie." He gets a thoughtful look now. "But I think you were wrong to quit the team."

"Coach thought I was wrong too."

"Did you tell him why?"

"No way!"

"Does anyone else know about it?"

I nod. "Lauren Kempt knows. She saw Jess going to that gay alliance meeting last week. She figured it out."

"She's not gay too, is she?"

"No, not at all. Although I have to admit I wondered the same thing. But then we talked, and I could tell she's not."

"Well, you know what they say about those sports-jock girls."

"Don't say that, Mitch. I'm one of those girls too, you know."

He smiles. "No, you're not."

"I am," I insist. "I do volleyball and basketball and soccer and—"

"I know." He nods with approval. "And I've seen you in that volleyball outfit and, trust me, no sports-jock girl looks anything like that."

I feel my cheeks getting warm, and I pick up my unfinished food and carry it toward the sink.

"Hey, you're not throwing that out, are you?"

I turn and look at him. "You want it?"

"You bet!"

I laugh as I take my plate back to him. "Help yourself."

"So, what are you going to do about all this?" he asks as he puts my sandwich on his plate and tops off his soup with my leftovers.

"What can I do?"

"I don't know." He dips his sandwich again. "But I don't think you can just roll over and let it take you out."

"I've really been praying for Jess. And this afternoon I sent her the website for this exit group where Christians counsel homosexuals back to the truth."

"The truth?"

"You know, that homosexuality is wrong."

"How do you know for sure that it is?"

"Because of the Bible." I say with a little impatience, studying Mitch's expression and wondering whether he really is a Christian.

"Do you think that homosexuals can really change who they are?"

"I read lots of testimonies. You know, from people who used to be gay and then turned straight. They sounded pretty convincing to me. So I think God can change people, if people want to change, that is."

"I know my dad would probably agree with you on that. But I'm just not so sure myself. I'm not convinced that people aren't just born that way, and that's the way it is."

Okay, this response disappoints me a little. I wish that Mitch had stronger convictions about something like this. But then I suppose he's just being honest. And maybe it's just something he needs to give a little more thought to. "Well, that just figures," I say. "I agree with your dad and you agree with my mom."

He laughs, then says, "Hey, sounds like we could be one big happy family," which makes me laugh too. And, while I know Mitch isn't exactly proposing marriage (that would be scary), it does make me feel like we have a future, at least a dating future. For the first time since last Saturday, I feel like maybe I will survive this thing after all. I think maybe there's hope. Thank God for Mitch!

nine

"THANKS FOR PICKING ME UP," I TELL MITCH THE NEXT MORNING.

"No problem," he says as he pulls out of my driveway.

"Sure beats taking the bus." I laugh. "Okay, that's a huge understatement. This is like way, way better than taking the bus!"

"Hey, I understand. I used to have to ride the bus sometimes too. I was so glad when I finally got my own wheels."

"Yeah, if you hadn't offered me a lift, I probably would've started riding my bike to school," I admit.

"That might be a challenge when it gets icy."

"Well, I really do appreciate it. And if I get a job, like I plan to, maybe I'll have wheels too, before long anyway. Maybe by Christmas even."

"You still stuck on that idea?"

"Why not?"

"Well, it just seems such a waste."

"Getting a car?" I turn and stare at Mitch. It worries me that he sometimes reminds me of my mom—not something you really want to see in your boyfriend!

"No, not that. Getting a car is cool. I mean giving up basketball just because Jess is gay. It just seems like such a waste."

"Oh."

"I mean you're so talented, Ramie. Really, if I was as good as you, I'd try out for the guys' team. And the way they're looking this year, they might even take me."

"The guys' team does seem to be in need of help."

"Seriously, Ramie, don't you want to rethink this whole quitting thing?"

"I don't see how."

He gives me his best pep talk, and there are moments when I think he could be right, but by the time we get to school, I just can't get into it.

"The truth is, I think it'd be selfish for me to stay on the team," I finally decide as we get out of his car. "I mean I was never that into basketball before. I hadn't even played on a real team since middle school. But Jess totally loves basketball. She always has. I think she actually likes it better than softball. She goes to basketball camp every summer and she watches every men's and women's game she can find on ESPN. She's a basketball junkie. And she's the one who talked me into trying out this year. If I stay on the team, it can only create problems between us, and for everyone else. My guess is that she would end up quitting."

"So . . ."

"So, Jess has made a humongous mistake in becoming a lesbian, and it's a mistake she's going to suffer for, especially if people find out. But for her to lose basketball on top of that? Well, I just don't want to be the one responsible for that kind of pain. Okay?"

As we walk, Mitch puts his arm around my shoulders and pulls me toward him in a tight squeeze. "You're really a nice person, Ramie. You know that?"

I make a face at him. "Not as nice as you might think. I mean I can say this stuff and maybe it sounds good, but the truth is, there's a part of me that would happily go back out for the team and play my best and be sort of glad if Jess went down. I mean if it just would make her rethink all this homosexual crud, I'm sure I'd do it."

"So, what if that was the case? Why not just go for it then?"

"Because it feels too mean. Okay?"

He smiles at me. "Okay."

We walk into school like this, with his arm around me, and I am so glad, and I don't care who sees us. In fact, I hope everyone sees us! It would make life so much easier if Mitch and I appeared to be an established couple. Just in case any word about Jess leaks out. Not that it will. But just in case. As I see kids I know, I kind of nod and smile and say hey, like this is no big deal. Like Ramie Grant always has a good-looking guy with his arm around her.

"Can I walk you to class?" he offers after I make a quick stop at my new locker.

"Sure, if you want." This is a very welcome surprise, since several of my friends have U.S. History first period too. Including Jess. And this gives me another opportunity to be seen with "my boyfriend."

We pause by the open door to the classroom to say good-bye, and then Mitch leans forward and gives me a quick kiss on the lips. It's our third *real* kiss so far. One on the first date, one when he left last night, and now! Oh, he's given me a few pecks here and there, on the forehead and cheeks. But this kiss, right here in public, is a real attention getter for a girl like me. And as I walk into class, I can see that several people, including Jess, were watching us.

Okay, I'll admit that I've always been the kind of person who made fun of public displays of affection. If I saw someone making out in the hallway, I'd usually make a face and sometimes even say something as lame as, "Get a room, why don't ya?" But the rules have changed now. And I realize that I must change too. Change is good, right?

So I hold my head tall as I walk into class, taking a seat about halfway up, in the same row as Lauren and BJ.

"Whoa," says BJ. "Guess I was right about you and Mitch after all."

I try to act nonchalant. "Yeah, didn't I tell you that we went out Sunday night?"

She looks surprised. "No, you didn't. Man, you work fast, Ramie."

"Yeah," says Lauren in this cynical tone. "This girl is just *full* of surprises."

BJ frowns at me. "Yeah, what's the deal, Ramie?"

"Huh?"

"Skipping practice yesterday? What's up with that?"

"I, uh, I didn't exactly skip, BJ. Didn't Coach tell you guys?"

"Tell us what?" demands Lauren.

"That I quit."

"You *what?*" BJ looks seriously shocked now and Lauren looks furious. But Mr. Hyde is already up in front and class is beginning. And, as we all know, this guy will not tolerate "visiting in class." Mr. Hyde starts droning on about the post-Civil War era, and I can feel BJ staring at me, and I know that Lauren is livid. I guess I should've seen this coming. I suppose I've been a little distracted with Mitch. Still, it irks me that Coach Ackley never told the team that I quit. What's up with that anyway? But then I think I get it. I bet, like Mitch, Coach is still thinking he can talk me into staying. Too bad! He'll have to think again.

History is barely over when both BJ and Lauren practically jump on me, one on either side.

"Have you gone nuts?" BJ studies me as if she really does think I'm losing my mind. "You're the best player on the team. How can you just walk out like that?"

"Ramie," says Lauren with narrowed eyes. "If this is about what I think it is, you *cannot* do this. This is *not* fair."

"What do you mean?" BJ asks Lauren. "What do you think it is? What's not fair?"

"Ramie?" Lauren ignores BJ and puts a tight grip on my arm. "Is it?"

"Let go of me," I tell her, shaking my arm free. "What if it is? Don't I have a right to make my own decisions? Isn't it *my* life?"

"But you're letting us *all* down," Lauren says sadly. "And it's just because of . . ."

"What is going on?" demands BJ. She glances over my shoulder now, toward the back of the room where Jess had been sitting earlier. For all I know, she's still sitting there. "Is this about Jess?" asks BJ.

Lauren and I both turn around to see that Jess is in fact still sitting there. She's watching the three of us and wearing the same scared look that I saw on her face at practice yesterday. The old deer-caught-in-the-headlights expression—like is she going to run for her life or just take the hit?

But I am getting seriously fed up now. I'm tired of tiptoeing around and playing these games. And so I just look back at Jess and loudly say, "I don't know. *Is* this about Jess?"

She doesn't say a word, but now her expression is changing from scared to angry. I think she's about to really let me have it. I think she's about to tell me off. And I know she can do it. Jess, when infuriated, can speak her mind with no problem. I've heard her. But instead of lashing into me, she just stands, picks up her stuff, and walks out.

"What is going on?" demands BJ.

"*Ask Jess!*" I stand, grab my stuff and split, almost running to get away from them. But they're right on my heels, and I can hear BJ and Lauren bickering, and then BJ starts pestering me to tell her why I quit the team, and Lauren is nagging me to change my mind, but I just ignore them. I just keep walking faster and faster. But as I walk, I can feel myself getting madder and madder at my ex–best friend. This is her fault. She's the one who brought all this on. But it's like I'm the one who's getting tortured here. I'm the one with the friends who are turning against me. I'm the one who lost a spot on the team. I'm paying the price, but Jess is the one who's to blame. This is so wrong. So totally wrong. And then, just as I reach the science department and I think BJ and Lauren have temporarily given up on me, a light goes on in my head. Maybe this is how Jesus felt when people picked on him. Is it possible that I'm actually being perse-cuted for righteousness' sake? If that's the case, maybe I should just keep my mouth shut and bear it. *God make me strong,* I pray as I take my seat in chemistry. *God help me.*

This thought helps me to get through the rest of the morning, but by noon I feel slightly beat up. It seems like the whole school knows now that I quit the basketball team. Okay, that's probably an exaggeration. But the whole team knows. And it seems like every single one of them has aimed their sites at me today. Rumors are flying fast and furious now. Mostly the arrows are targeted at my relationship with Mitch. My ex-teammates, other than Lauren, are assuming I betrayed the team just so that I could have more time to spend with my new boyfriend. Yeah, right.

"How's it going?" Mitch asks, after he's caught me from behind, which wasn't much of a challenge since I was plodding toward the cafeteria as slowly as possible.

But I'm so relieved to see him that I throw my arms around him and hug him tightly. "I'm so happy to see you!"

He grins with surprise. "Cool. Is there any special reason you're so happy? Or is it just due to my sweet nature and general good looks?"

Then I give him the lowdown on my morning and how things just seem to be getting worse. I even explain the assumptions about how I quit the team because of him.

"That's crazy," he says. "If anything, I'm trying to talk you into staying on the team."

"Tell me about it."

"Maybe I should tell someone else about it."

"You mean start some *new* rumors?"

"Yeah, we could start all kinds of rumors. Just make up a bunch of stuff, toss it out there, and see if any of it sticks."

So we start joking about all the whacked-out rumors we could start, and before I know it I'm laughing. "You're good for me, Mitch," I tell him, but when we reach the cafeteria I stop in front of the door. I so do not want to go in there. I don't want to see BJ or Lauren or Amy or any of them.

"Wanna go someplace else for lunch?" he offers.

I turn and look at him. "But it's closed campus."

He gets this mischievous look. "But you can sneak out with me, if you want to. I'm officially checked out, you know, so I can take my car off the lot without getting into trouble."

"Yeah, maybe you can, but I might—"

"Hey, what do you have to lose?" He grabs me by the hand. "Maybe they'll even suspend you from the team for a couple of weeks."

I consider this. "Yeah. Maybe you're right." And so, even though I know it's wrong, I go with him. We dash over to the parking lot, and then I actually hunch down in his car, like I really think some school official is watching, although Mitch assures me that's not the case. "Don't worry," he says. "My friends and I used to sneak out for lunch all the time when we were juniors, and we never got caught."

Still, I stay down until he's a block or two from school. Then I pop up and start laughing. "This is kinda fun," I admit.

"And from what I hear of your mom, it's not like she'd get mad at you for something like this," he says. "She sounds pretty understanding to me."

I consider this. "Yeah, she'd probably give me a little talk about how it's my life and how the way I live it is up to me, but that I'm the one who will have to deal with the consequences. Stuff like that."

"But isn't that true?"

I think about this. "I guess so. But I also know I need to obey God. And part of obeying God is obeying the rules and respecting your parents and authority and stuff. But you know all about that. Your dad's probably instilled that into you since you—"

"Yeah, yeah." He kind of brushes this off like he doesn't want to talk about his dad. "So where's your dad in all this, Ramie? I mean I've heard a lot about your mom, but you never say a word about your dad. What's he like?"

"What's he like?" I slowly sink back into the seat as I contemplate on how to best answer Mitch. "It's kind of a long story," I say, hoping that might be the end of it.

"Okay, then let me treat you to lunch and you can tell me all about it."

So it is that we're sitting over cheeseburgers and mocha shakes and I start telling Mitch more about my dad than I've told anyone. Including Jess.

"I used to just think I didn't have a dad," I begin. "I mean I'd never actually seen him or anything. When I got old enough to realize that everyone has a dad, I asked my mom about him. At first she just told me that my dad lived in a different country, and I kind of accepted that."

"A different country?"

"Yeah, he's Jamaican. He came over here on an exchange program with my mom's parents' church. He was studying to become a pastor, and my grandparents were his host family. My mom was in her second year of college and, according to her, she had changed a lot after leaving home. You see, her parents were Christians, but extremely religious and extremely conservative, not cool like your parents. So as soon as my mom got away from them she went a little wild."

He chuckles. "That sounds familiar."

"Anyway, she said she had this need to rebel against them so that she could find herself, you know? By her second year of college she was smoking pot and drinking and doing pretty much anything she could think of that they wouldn't approve of, which didn't sound too difficult since they pretty much didn't approve of anything."

Mitch laughs. "Sounds kind of like what my older sister did when she went off to college. Man, my parents freaked big time. But after a couple of years, she straightened up. She married a pretty nice guy, and now everyone seems happy."

"Well, my mom never straightened up—at least not in the opinion of my grandparents. They're still estranged."

"Too bad."

"Maybe. Anyway, it was Christmas break and my mom went home to visit her parents. And that's when she met David, the aspiring pastor."

"The Jamaican exchange student?"

"Yeah. She and David kind of hit it off. My mom said he was really handsome, and she was really pretty then. Long blonde hair, blue eyes, good figure, you know. And they were attracted to each other."

"Uh-oh."

"Yeah. She's admitted to me that their little fling might've had as much to do with getting back at her parents as it did with liking David. But she also assured me it was mutual. Apparently she didn't have to do much to lead the poor man astray. Of course, she had never planned on getting pregnant."

"Her parents must've been fuming."

"She didn't tell them."

"Never?"

"Not for a long time. She went back to school and got a job to support herself, got some kind of assistance, and then just kept plugging along until she got her counseling degree."

"Wow, she must be a pretty strong person."

"Yeah, I guess so."

"So have you ever met your father?"

"Nope."

"Does that bug you?"

"Sometimes. Especially when I was about fourteen. For some reason I got totally obsessed over it. All I had of my father was this faded photograph that Mom gave me of this nice-looking dark-skinned guy standing in front of a Christmas tree. But he seemed like a perfect stranger. I told my mom that I had to meet him, and I almost talked her into letting me go to Jamaica that summer. But then she did a little research and found out that he had become a pastor after all, and he was married and had four children under the ages of seven. She helped me to understand that he hadn't really abandoned me, since he never knew I existed in the first place. And since I was a Christian by then, well, I decided I had to just forgive him and move on with my life."

"Wow."

I shrug. "It's no big deal, really. I mean it's just the way it is. You get used to it."

"What about your grandparents? Did you ever meet them?"

"Yeah. Mom took me out to meet them when I was eight, just before we moved to Greenville. I think she was actually hoping they'd welcome her with open arms, and maybe she'd find a job in her old hometown and we'd settle down there."

"But they didn't?"

"Not even close. It was pretty pathetic, really."

"Too bad."

"Yeah, I think it's too bad for them. They seem like they're trapped in this phony-baloney Christian world. I mean I'm a Christian too, but I sure don't want to be like them. You could tell they were embarrassed by us. Probably me mostly. Anyway, we couldn't get out of there quick enough." I take a final sip of my shake and glance at my watch. "Whoa, I better get back or I'm going to be late for French, and this time I don't have an excuse."

"Let's go," he says, standing quickly. "I'll drop you by the east wing. If you run, you can probably make it."

As I run in through a side door, Lauren spies me. She has French during fifth period too, although I was actually hoping to be late enough to avoid seeing her before class.

"Did Mitch take you to lunch?" she asks as we both jog toward the classroom.

"Yeah."

"Must be nice."

I glance at her. "Huh?"

"To keep people from thinking anything about you and Jess."

But now we're inside the class and it's too late to respond. Still, I find it hard to concentrate on conjugating verbs as I replay her little comment. Like what did she mean by that? And was it as bitter as it sounded? Finally, class is over and I take Lauren aside.

"What's up with what you said just before class?" I ask.

She glares at me now. "It's like you're just running away from everything, Ramie. And you're leaving me all by myself, just holding the bag."

"Holding the bag? What's that supposed to mean?"

"It means that I'm the only one, besides you, who knows about Jess's . . . you know, her lesbian thing. How am I supposed to feel?"

"I don't know." I stare at her. "How *are* you supposed to feel?" What I want to say is, *What does this have to do with me? Why is this still my problem?* I mean she can't possibly think that I'm personally responsible for Jess, can she?

"I don't know what to do, Ramie," she says, her voice softening some.

"You don't have to *do* anything," I point out.

"You mean the way *you* haven't done anything?" she says, her anger reigniting. "Like you didn't quit the team, like you didn't run out and get a boyfriend, like you're not avoiding all your old friends now? Sheesh, why don't you just change your name and assume a whole new identity?"

"It's not like that."

"Yeah, right."

I really do not deserve this kind of abuse. "Well, I've got to get going, or I'm going to be late to health class."

"You can't get off this easy, Ramie," she yells after me. And I wonder what that's supposed to mean. *Easy?* Like who is she kidding? I feel like I'm walking a tightrope backward and blindfolded with both hands tied behind my back. How is that supposed to be easy?

ten

By the end of the day, I am drained. All I can think is that I want to go home. I don't even care that I'm not on the basketball team, that I'm not going to practice. All I want is an escape. I don't even mind that I'll be riding the stupid school bus. Anything to get out of this place.

I sit close to the door during English, my last class of the day, ready to bolt. Joey Pinckney is sitting in the chair opposite me, on the other side of the door, and he's looking pretty uncomfortable. I suspect that he's preparing to dash out of here too. Maybe it'll be a contest to see who will get out the door first. I wonder if people have heard about him going to the gay alliance meeting too. Is he taking some heat about it? And does his going mean that he's gay too? I look away, asking myself why I should care.

My main reason for wanting to make a quick exit is because Lauren and Amy are in this class too, and judging by the way they keep glancing at each other, then looking back at me, I suspect they plan to nab me if they can. But I'm a step ahead of them. I already stopped by my locker to get what I need so that I can make a fast break and get out of school altogether.

I keep my eye on the clock and as soon as the second hand goes straight up, before the final bell even starts to ring, I am up and outta there, sprinting down the hall. Pinckney never had a chance. I can see the side door now, the one that I've already chosen to use for my speedy exodus, when I hear a familiar voice.

"Ramie!" she yells. Although I know it's Jess, I'm surprised that she's calling my name. Even though I'm slightly curious as to why, I just keep on going, making it almost to the door.

"Ramie!" she yells again, even louder. "Wait!"

Something in me breaks now. I mean Jess is going through some hard stuff right now. Maybe she's even rethinking this whole thing. Maybe God is finally answering my prayers. So I stop and, catching my breath, I wait.

"We need to talk," she says when she reaches me.

"Okay." I hold my backpack in front of my chest, almost as if it's a shield, and wait for her to say something.

"Why are you doing this?" she finally asks me.

"Huh?"

"Why are you making everything so hard?"

"Me?"

"And I know that you've told people." Her eyes narrow in anger.

"I have *not!*"

"Lauren knows."

"But she—"

"And BJ acts like—"

"I never—"

"Why are you doing this to me, Ramie?" She's using an overly loud voice now, one that's sure to draw attention. "We used to be friends. And now you're treating me like—"

"It's not my fault," I tell her. "You're the one who—"

"I thought I could trust you!" she yells. "I thought you were my friend!"

88

I can tell that others are watching us now. I even see Joey's pale, worried face off to one side, not really part of the crowd, but not leaving either. Then I glance to my right and see that Amy and Lauren are about ten feet away, and then BJ joins them. It seems like everyone is just frozen in time, like they're all just waiting, as if they expect to see some kind of showdown.

"I *was* your friend," I say quietly to Jess. "But you've changed. And that changes everything. Can't you see that?"

"No!" she yells at me, her dark eyes bright with anger as she shakes her finger in my face. "You're the one who's changed, Ramie! I trusted you! And you *outted* me!"

I'm sure I look shocked now. Like does she know what she's saying? Does she know that people are listening? *"Jess!"* I say in warning, like, *Think about this, think about what you're saying here.*

But she just shakes her head. "I don't care what people think anymore. I don't have anything to hide." Then she turns around and looks at the spectators and yells. "Yeah, that's right, I'm gay! I'm a homosexual! I'm a lesbian! There! I'm out of the closet! Are you all happy now? Is this what everyone was waiting for? Do you want to take me outside and beat me up now? Do you want to start throwing rocks at me? Do you want to—" And then her face just cracks, like she can't control it, and suddenly she is crying.

"Jess?" I say in a shaky voice as she stands there, just a few feet away from me but all alone in the center of the hallway. She's bent over and holding her arms around her midsection as if someone has just shot her in the stomach, loudly sobbing. I've never seen Jess cry like this before, and it's kind of scary. I'm still clutching my backpack to my chest, but I know that I should just drop it, that I should go over and put my arms around her and that I should tell her I'm sorry and that I still love her and that I care about her. But it's like my feet are stuck to the floor. I can't move, I can't speak. I just can't.

"Jess," says Lauren in a compassionate voice, as she slowly comes toward her the way someone might approach a rabid dog. "It's going to be okay—"

"No!" Jess looks up at her and then at me with a tear-streaked face. "It is *not* okay. It's never going to be okay." And then she takes off running in the opposite direction, toward the locker bay.

"Should I follow her?" asks Lauren.

"I . . . I don't know." I'm still trying to process what has just happened, trying to decide if it's reality or just a bad dream.

"She probably just needs to chill," says Amy, who has stepped up next to Lauren now, putting her hand on her shoulder in an encouraging way.

"Wow," says BJ as she joins us. "I never saw that one coming."

"I knew about it," says Lauren.

"Those athletic girls," says a girl from the group of spectators that's just starting to break up. "I always knew they were a bunch of lesbians."

"Watch what you say around the jock-chicks!" says someone else. "They might beat you up." Naturally, this is followed by peals of laughter and several more crude jokes that I try to block out.

"You guys are total idiots!" yells Amy.

"Yeah, why don't you get a life," says BJ.

"And grow up while you're at it!" adds Lauren.

"Come on, Ramie," says BJ as she grabs me by the arm. The next thing I know they're all herding me down toward the gym and then into the girls' locker room, where they usher me through the door and into the small office that's used by the PE teachers, who fortunately aren't around at the moment.

"Maybe it will be private in here," says BJ.

"Like it's going to matter," says Lauren.

The four of us cram inside, standing in a circle around the desk, and just look at each other. I can tell that we're all still kind of in shock.

"So, *that's* why you quit the team." Amy is looking at me now.

I nod.

"I told her not to," says Lauren.

"Yeah, if anyone should quit, it should be Jess," says Amy. "She's the one who's messed everything up."

"That's not fair," says Lauren. "Just because she's gay doesn't mean she can't be on the team. That's wrong."

"But won't it feel weird?" says Amy. "I mean I sure don't want to strip down in front of her anymore."

I glance out to the locker room, where girls are in various stages of dress and undress, completely oblivious as to whether they're being watched as they get ready for basketball practice. We take so much for granted.

"So, are you afraid that Jess's going to come on to you, Amy?" Lauren teases her best friend.

But Amy just glares at her. "No! It just makes me uncomfortable."

"I sort of know what you mean," I tell Amy. "It kind of creeps me out."

"Yeah, we probably all feel like that," admits BJ. "But then it's not like this is anything new either. I mean we've all been around Jess for a long time now. It's not like she's ever done anything weird to anyone." Then she looks curiously at me. *"Has she?"*

"No!" I firmly shake my head. "She has *never* done anything weird to me. Well, besides telling me about this. That was pretty bizarre."

91

"Yeah," says Lauren. "Ramie told me that she was as shocked as anyone when she heard the news."

"So, what are we going to do?" asks BJ.

"Do?" I echo. "What do you mean? What can we do?"

"I mean what are we going to do about Jess?"

"I don't think she should be on the team anymore," says Amy firmly.

"It's not like we can kick her off," says Lauren. "I mean just because she's a lesbian doesn't mean she doesn't have any rights."

"That's true," agrees BJ. "In fact, I think she could sue the school if she got kicked off the team for being homosexual. I'll bet she could get the ACLU in here like that." BJ snaps her fingers.

"Okay, so we can't kick her off," says Amy, "but we can make her *want* to quit."

"Jess loves basketball," I remind them.

BJ looks out the window into the locker room, peering around. "She might love basketball, but she's not out there now."

"That's because she was traumatized," I say.

"Yeah," says Lauren. "She'll probably be here. Maybe she'll come out late."

"Maybe we should get ready too," says BJ.

So we all go back into the locker room now, but as my friends head for their lockers, I go straight for the exit.

"Hey, where you going, Ramie?" demands Lauren as she runs over to stop me.

"Home."

"No way!" says BJ, as she joins us.

"But I quit," I remind them. "I already told Coach and—"

"That was yesterday," says Amy. "Before everyone knew about Jess."

Now the locker room gets noticeably quiet, and we turn around to see that all the other girls have stopped talking and dressing and are tuned in to us. And it's obvious that they all know what's going on. But now they're watching and waiting, like they want to see how we're going to handle this thing. I can especially feel them staring at me, like they're asking themselves whether I, like Jess, am also lesbian.

"Come on, Ramie," urges Lauren.

"Yeah," says Amy. "Don't let Jess ruin your life."

"We need you on the team," says Lauren.

"Your quitting isn't going to help Jess anyway," BJ points out. "Jess is going to have to sort out her own life."

"Maybe you're right," I agree.

"Of course, we're right," says BJ.

"Jess is the one who's messed up," says Amy. "Just because she's your friend doesn't mean you have to suffer for her."

And so I rethink yesterday's decision to quit, and BJ offers to loan me her extra practice uniform, and we all hurry to dress down, joining the others as we jog out to the court where Coach Ackley starts to bark out some drill instructions. Then just as I get a ball, he yells at me.

"Get over here, Grant!"

I run over to where he's standing on the sidelines. "Coach?"

"I heard about LeCroix."

"What?"

"Oh, don't kid yourself, the whole school will know all about this business by tomorrow. This stuff happens, Grant. But you can't let it stop you." Then he slaps me on the back. "Glad to see you're bigger than that. Glad to have you back."

"But what about Jess?" I ask.

He shrugs, then glances down at his clipboard. "What about her?"

"Uh, some of the girls are, well, uncomfortable, you know? And it might be hard on the team."

"Look, Grant. A long time ago, I was in the army. Back when they still had that don't-ask-don't-tell policy. You know what I mean?"

I nod.

"Well, that's how I'd like to keep things here. Okay? You girls sort this trouble out among yourselves. I won't ask. You don't tell. Got me?"

"I guess."

"Good."

So we start practicing, and I keep one eye on the locker-room door, expecting Jess to slip out at any time, but she never does. And I have to admit this concerns me some. But maybe Amy was right. Maybe Jess just needs some time to chill. Missing one practice isn't going to hurt her. It sure didn't hurt me. I've been playing harder than ever today.

"I'm so happy you're back," says BJ as we head back to the locker room.

"Me too!" Amy slaps me on the back. "You were shooting about 90 percent out there, Ramie!"

"You keep that up when season starts and we'll make it to state."

I feel kind of surprised at how many other players are glad to see me back too. I mean, they could resent me or blame me or even think that both Jess and I are bad news. But that doesn't seem the case. And suddenly I realize that quitting would've been a big mistake. Especially after Jess outed herself in front of everyone today. What good would it do the team to lose both of us? Not that Jess is not coming back. I'm sure she won't be giving up basketball for good.

The yelling and teasing seem louder than usual in the showers tonight. I'm not sure if everyone's just letting off steam after what went down with Jess or what. But, despite the jokes and craziness, I suspect that we're all a little uneasy beneath the surface. And I wonder how it's going to feel when Jess returns to practice. How will the girls act then?

"Need a ride home, Ramie?" asks BJ as she pulls on a sweatshirt.

I toss a pathetic smile her way. "I know it's out of your way."

"That's okay."

"Well, it's that or the activities bus," I admit.

"Not the dreaded *activities bus*," says Amy in mock horror. "Is there anything worse that that?"

I want to say yes. Riding home with Jess tonight would be worse. But then Jess is not here. I don't need to worry. Still, I wonder if she'll ever offer me rides again, once she comes back. And, if she does, what will I say?

"Do you think someone should call Jess?" BJ asks as she drives me home. "I mean just to make sure she's okay? She seemed pretty stressed today."

"Yeah. I was kinda worried about her too."

"Are you going to call her?"

"I, uh, I don't know." I twist the strap of my backpack. "It's hard, BJ, it's like I get all flustered and I don't know what to say to her. And I don't want to get into another fight with her, you know?"

"Maybe I should call her."

"Would you?"

"Yeah. It's not like I have the same history with her as you do. Besides, I think it's the Christian thing to do, you know. Like Pastor Bryant says, love the sinner, hate the sin. I think I can do that."

"Thanks, BJ." She's pulling up to my house now. "And thanks for the ride too. I'll be praying for your conversation with Jess tonight."

"Thanks. Want me to call you and let you know how it goes?"

"Sure," I tell her as I climb out of her VW Bug. But as I walk up the steps to the townhouse, I'm wishing that she wouldn't. I so want to be out of this picture, to be removed from anything that has anything to do with Jess. It's like everything in my life seems to be revolving around her right now. Will I ever escape her? All I want to do is forget all about her, forget that she and I were ever friends, wipe away every old memory, and erase the creepy confession that she made in the hallway at school today.

I just want out.

eleven

WEDNESDAY, I HEAR PLENTY OF OTHERS TALKING ABOUT JESS AROUND school—mostly the school idiots who really should get a life. There is a lot of talk, a lot of speculation. But, to my surprise, not everything said is negative. Some kids are pretty understanding and accepting, saying that it's no big deal and that everyone should get over it. I have to remind myself these kids probably aren't Christians. Like my mom, they have a worldly way of measuring sin: If it feels good, it must be okay.

Thankfully I have Mitch to lean on. He is relieved, for my sake, that I changed my mind about quitting. I think he is also relieved that this thing with Jess is out in the open now, and it doesn't seem to bother him that he's dating a girl whose ex–best friend is a lesbian. I think this helps everyone else to accept that I'm not like Jess. At least I hope so.

BJ is the only one who's talked to her since Tuesday's disaster, and BJ says it was pretty much like talking to a stone. But she says she'll keep trying. I'm trying not to feel guilty for bowing out. That's how it feels. Like I've totally stepped out of Jess's picture. If I see her at school today, though I haven't caught sight of her yet, I'll just look the other way. I am so grateful this is Thanksgiving week. A three-day week!

"Want to come to midweek service with me tonight?" Mitch asks me before he leaves at lunchtime.

"Sure," I say with surprise. "I didn't know that you usually went."

"I don't. But I promised my mom that I would. It's a special Thanksgiving service, you know, a family time." He kind of laughs. "Maybe your mom would like to join us."

"Yeah, right." Just the same, I decide to ask her anyway. And I decide that it's time for her to meet Mitch.

I'm not surprised that Mom politely declines my invitation. But she does want to meet Mitch, and when I invite him in, she seems to hit it off with him, and I think she might actually approve. Not that she would tell me if she didn't. It is, after all, my life. Still, it's kind of nice that she likes him.

"Have fun," she says as we head for the door. "If you can, that is." She laughs. "Church and fun existed in two different universes when I was a kid."

"You'll have to give it a second chance someday," I tell her.

"Yeah, yeah. I'll keep that in mind." She waves and we leave.

The first people I see when we walk into church are Jess's parents. They're standing by the door that leads to the sanctuary, and it almost feels as if they're waiting for me. I tell myself this is ridiculous, not to mention slightly paranoid. But as I get closer, they keep standing there, looking at me. At least Mrs. LeCroix is looking at me. Mr. LeCroix keeps his eyes on his shoes.

Now, I am totally unprepared for this. I suppose I have just blocked the possibility of this kind of encounter out of my mind. In a way, it feels like I've divorced Jess, and like I want to divorce her family too. But when I get close enough to really see their faces, I feel their sadness, and I can tell that they know.

Mrs. LeCroix forces a little smile for me. "Hello, Ramie. How are you doing?"

"Okay." I glance around, curious as to whether Jess is here.

"She's not here," says Mrs. LeCroix in a quiet tone.

"Oh."

"We *know*," she tells me.

"I'm sorry," I say in return, unsure if that is the right response. It almost feels as if I'm at a funeral, like Jess really is dead and no one knows what to say. It's weird.

"This is very hard," she says.

"I know."

"Did you . . . did you know about this?"

"You mean before just recently, when she decided to come out—out of the closet, I mean?"

She nods. "Yes, did you know?"

I shake my head. "I was just as shocked as you."

Then she reaches over and takes my hand. "So, you're not like that then?"

"No!" Then I lower my voice. "Not at all."

She reaches into her purse for a tissue and then blots a stray tear.

I have no idea what I should say, what I should do, but I can feel others waiting behind us, and I suspect we're causing a traffic jam. "Maybe we can talk later," I tell her.

"Yes. Maybe after the service, if you have time." She dabs her nose with the tissue, and Mitch and I move on.

Mitch's hand slips beneath my elbow as we walk down the center aisle, and it's such a comforting feeling. Then, to my surprise, Mitch leads us all the way to the front, where he guides us into the pew next to his mom and family. They lean over and smile at me and say hello, and not for the first time I think, *Thank God for Mitch!*

It's a good service, but I'm afraid that most of it is flying right over my head. I'm too focused on that unsettling conversation with Jess's mom and the knowledge that it's not finished yet. And then there is Mitch sitting next to me, occasionally reaching over and giving my hand a squeeze, with his family right here too. I can't help but wonder what they think of me. I wonder if they've heard about Jess. Does the whole church know, and if so, what do they think? Do they assume the worst about me? I am totally on emotional overload just now. I wish I could sneak outside and just chill.

Finally the service is done and I tell Mitch that I promised to talk to Mrs. LeCroix again. "Do you mind?"

He smiles. "Not at all."

So I go to find her and she asks me to sit down. "I don't know what to do, Ramie," she says, looking into my eyes as if she might find some answers there. "You know that we believe homosexuality is a sin. Jessica knows this too. But I don't know what to do." And then she really starts to cry.

"I don't know what to do either," I tell her. But then I remember the website I found and the name of the exit ministry. So I tell her about it. "Maybe you could contact someone there," I suggest. "Someone who understands this stuff."

"It's so hard to know why some people . . . well, why anyone would want to do something like that, to be like that. And then when it's your own daughter, and you love her, but you despise what she's doing . . . I think I must've done something wrong. Maybe we should've discouraged her about sports." She's wringing her hands now, and I reach over and pat her on the arm.

"It's not your fault," I assure her. Then I remind her of my mom and how liberal she is and how I've become such the opposite by being a Christian. "My mom thinks that what Jess is doing is perfectly fine and normal."

"Maybe we should simply switch children," she says with a trace of lightness in her voice.

I try to laugh. "Somehow we're going to get through this," I tell her. "I'm still praying for Jess."

"I'll tell Gary about that ministry," she says. "Thank you. I don't want to take up your time. I see that you came with Mitch Bryant. He seems like such a nice young man."

I smile. "He is."

"Well, have a happy Thanksgiving, Ramie."

"You too."

She frowns. "The other kids don't know about this yet. Jess plans to tell them tomorrow. I doubt if anyone will have much of an appetite after that."

"Sorry."

She nods.

I go to find Mitch, but as I walk through the thinning crowd in the church I can tell that some people are looking at me. And I'm not sure if it's because of what they may have heard about Jess or because I'm here with Mitch, or maybe I'm just getting really para-noid. But I hold my head high as I walk and I pray that we can leave soon. I am so worn out from all this.

"Got any big plans for Thanksgiving?" Mitch asks as he drives me home after church.

"Nothing much," I admit. "My mom and I usually go to her friends' place and hang out with some of her counseling buddies. How about you?"

"We're heading up to Newburg, the grandparents. Family tradi-tion stuff, you know, like aunts telling me how tall I've grown, uncles asking me what I plan to do with my life, crying babies who need to be bounced, and old people falling asleep after dinner. We'll be back on Saturday."

"Sounds nice."

"It gets old."

I don't tell him that I'd gladly trade that pleasant image for hanging out with a bunch of freaky counselor types who for one reason or another seem to be cut off from their families. Funny that family counselors aren't better able to deal with their own family problems. Makes you wonder how they can help anyone.

As usual, Mitch walks me to the front door. And, as usual, he kisses me. But instead of limiting him to just one kiss, we stand there and kiss for a while. And when we stop, I am lightheaded and it feels like everything is spinning.

"Wow," he says, stepping back with a slightly dazed look.

"Wow," I say back, wondering if he's feeling the same way I am.

"Doing anything on Saturday?" he asks.

"We have basketball practice in the morning," I tell him. "Our first preseason game is next week."

"I mean Saturday *night*."

"No. I'm not doing anything. I mean since there's no youth group because of the holiday weekend, otherwise I'd be doing something."

So he asks me out, and I say yes, then we kiss again, and I go in the house without even feeling the floor beneath my feet. *Wow* is right!

twelve

THANKSGIVING PASSES UNEVENTFULLY. SAME OLD SAME OLD. I FIND MYSELF daydreaming about what it would be like to be with Mitch, to be doing the "traditional" thing with his family. It sounds so good. Finally it's time to go home.

Mom works on updating some files, and I go to my room and check e-mail. I guess I'm hoping that Mitch might e-mail me. But I'm surprised to see that Jess has written. She's left the subject space blank and I feel nervous as I click the message open, preparing myself for the worst, though it might be good news.

> i know u r mad at me. and i feel the same. but maybe we shud talk. r u willing? Jess

Okay, that was pretty brief and to the point. But how do I react? Do I want to talk? No, not really. But is it right to just brush her off? After thinking this through, I bite the bullet and write back.

> i'm not mad. not really. just kinda confused. like y r u doing this? r u sure u r really gay? stuff like that. i just don't get u. sorry. ramie

I hit send and just sit there staring at the screen. I really don't want to have this conversation with her. I would rather just pretend that I don't know her. Never did. But one of the things I did manage to pick up out of Pastor Bryant's sermon last night was that Thanksgiving is a time of relationships, and relationships are about forgiveness. And I knew that I needed to forgive Jess. But how do you do that? I mean when the other person isn't asking for forgiveness. How do you forgive someone who thinks they are right and you are wrong? As I sit there thinking these thoughts, I see that Jess has replied. She's obviously sitting in front of her computer too. Now part of me thinks this is kind of silly, like we should probably just pick up the phone and call, talk in person. But I'm not ready for that. Maybe this is easier. I open her mail and read.

> i know it's hard to get. but i am gay. okay? that's
> just how it is. u need to get over it. i miss u. Jess

Gulp. How am I supposed to take that? Does she miss me as her friend? Or does she miss me like . . . like a girlfriend? Did Jess like me for me or was it something—ugh—more? This is so creepy. But maybe it's best to just get the crud out on the table. Clear things up. Or else make it clear that I don't want any kind of involvement with her at all.

> i miss u 2. but i miss the old u. i miss just being
> friends, having someone to hang with. i don't
> get this new u. i don't like that u r gay. i want
> things to be the way they were. y r u gay? do u
> even know? and how do u know u r gay? all of
> this is confusing to me. and frustrating. ramie

I wait to see if she'll respond. And as I wait I think I might've offended her. But I don't really care. I'm just being honest. If she can't take it, fine. We don't have to talk. I mean I am so ready to move on. But then her next post appears in my box, and I hurry to open it.

> i know i am gay. i knew it a long time ago. i just never cud face it b4. it's not easy facing it now. and friends like you and the others don't make it any easier. i wish u guys cud understand. i wish u cud accept me 4 myself. u don't know how hard this is 4 me. sometimes i wish i was dead. Jess

Okay, this scares me a little. The line about wishing she was dead is kind of freaky. But then I wonder, is she just saying this to manipulate me? Is this her way of guilting me into accepting her sin?

> if this is so hard and making u so miserable that u wish u were dead, y do u want to do it? y do u want to be gay? can't u see it's a big fat mess? can't u see that it's sin? i talked to ur mom yesterday. she is so upset. this hurts everyone, Jess, can't u see that? did u get my e-mail last week, about the exit ministry for homosexuals? maybe they can help u. y not talk to them? maybe it's not 2 late. ramie

I say a prayer as I hit send. *Please, God, please help her to see that this is wrong, please help her to see that she needs help.* I pray and pray until I see that she's e-mailed back again. I feel hopeful as I open it.

u just don't get it. u don't get me. it's no use trying to make u understand. u never will. y don't u go get help, ramie? u r the one who is all mixed up. being a homosexual is not a choice. it's how we are made. don't blame me, blame god. he made me like this. although i'm not sure i believe in god now that everyone who claims to be a christian is turning against me. i don't know what i believe. but i know it's no use talking to people like u. just leave me alone, okay? Jess

Okay, I can take a hint. Without answering her, I sign off of my e-mail and log off my computer. If she doesn't want to talk to me, fine. It's not like I wanted to talk to her in the first place anyway. And she's right, I don't understand her. I probably never will. Most of all, I just want to forget her. I almost wish she'd transfer to another high school. Maybe she will. Maybe she can find a gay school to go to, a place where everyone will understand her.

The day after Thanksgiving, I spend a pretty boring day at home. After trying to connect with both BJ and Lauren and finding that both of them aren't home, I decide to catch up on homework, comforting myself with the fact that I'll be going out with Mitch tomorrow night.

Saturday, I am actually relieved to go to practice. So relieved that I don't even mind riding my bike to the school. Fortunately the weather has warmed up a little. The sun is out and it's actually a pretty nice day. But the ride takes longer than I expected and now I'm running late. At least I'm warmed up and ready to play. I park and lock my bike in front of the main entrance to the gym.

I hurry toward the door, stripping off my jacket as I go inside. But as I turn down the hallway that goes past the restrooms, I see Jess just ahead of me. With her gym bag in hand, she's going into the girls' locker room. I freeze, wondering what I should do. I'm probably just late enough that the rest of the team is already dressed down and at practice. And I do not want to be alone with Jess in the locker room. Okay, it's not like I'm afraid of her or anything. I'm not. But I do know it will be really uncomfortable in there. For both of us.

I decide to go directly to the gym, where I find the rest of the team already doing drills.

"Sorry, I'm late," I tell the coach. "I, uh, had to ride my bike and it took longer than—"

"Just get dressed down, Grant. And hurry!"

"But I, uh—"

"No ifs ands or buts. Get moving, you hear?"

I swallow and nod, then start walking toward the girls' locker room.

"Get a move on!" he yells.

So I jog over to the door and open it and practically hold my breath as I quietly go inside. Jess is just pulling on a practice jersey, but she jumps when she hears the door to the gym slam shut behind me.

"Oh," she says, glaring at me. "It's you."

"Yeah," I say, looking away. "I'm late." Then instead of going for my locker, which is only a few feet from where she is dressing, I go straight to the bathroom and into a stall.

"You going in there to hurl?" she asks in a bitter-sounding voice.

"No," I say in a deliberate but cold tone. "I rode my bike over here and I need to use the toilet, if you don't mind."

Of course, I don't really need to go, but I just stand there and then flush and go out and slowly wash my hands, waiting until I can see by the reflection in the mirror that she is heading out to the gym. Then I dash over to my locker and dress down as fast as I can, hurrying out to the gym just a couple minutes after her.

I can feel the other players looking curiously at me as I fall into the drill patterns. But, even more than that, I can see they are looking at Jess. And it almost looks like some of them are (1) trying to avoid her, or (2) throwing the ball harder than necessary when they pass to her. A small part of me feels sorry for her, and I wonder why she came today.

Finally we're done with drills and Coach has just organized us into two scrimmage teams. But then he eyes Jess. "You're back, LeCroix?"

"Yes, sir."

"Do you plan to stick around for the whole season or is this just some kind of hit-and-miss thing for you?"

"I plan to stick around."

"Well, you know that missing practice last week means you'll be suspended for the first preseason game, don't you?"

"I know."

He shrugs. "Okay." He blows his whistle. "Let's play ball."

Jess and I are on opposite teams. She, as usual, is playing guard and, as usual, is pretty tight on defense. Today, I'm playing center, but I really prefer forward, since I'm probably the best outside shooter on the team. But Coach has made it clear he wants us to master all the positions. And so I work hard to keep myself in and around the key, shooting when I get the chance. At the same time it seems that Jess is working extra hard to keep me out of the key and from shooting. I know that's what she's supposed to do, but several times she fouls me and a couple of them seem intentional. In fact, if this was a real game, I'm sure she'd be sitting on the sidelines by now.

"Knock it off!" Lauren yells at Jess after I take a hit that knocks me to the floor.

"Yeah," says BJ, who is actually on Jess's scrimmage team. "Take it easy, Jess. This isn't WWF you know."

Then Coach finally gets a clue, blows his whistle, and takes Jess out for a while. During this time, both teams play hard and fast, but the tension factor seems to lighten a little. Then, as we're closing in, and it looks like my team will have a sure win, Coach sends Jess back in. I try not to think about it, reminding myself that this could happen in a real game, that someone on the opposing team could take a strong dislike to me and try to make me suffer.

"Okay, now let's see some good defense!" Coach yells as Lauren is dribbling down court and I'm making a sprint for the key. Then, just as I get into position, Lauren makes a great pass. I go up for what looks like a sure shot and *bam!* I am hit from behind by what feels like a linebacker or maybe a Toyota pickup. The ball goes flying from my hands and I go straight down. I use my left hand to block my fall, but it seems to give out on me and I continue to plunge, smacking my forehead right into the floor. I think I see stars.

"Are you okay?" asks Lauren, who is standing over me now.

I sit up, holding my left arm in front of me. It looks a little crooked, or maybe it's just that my vision is impaired from the whack on the head. "What happened?" I ask.

"Jess ran into you," says BJ, who is also standing over me. She turns and glares at Jess, who is standing a few feet away and looking on with what seems like genuine concern.

"On purpose!" snaps Lauren.

"It was not," says Jess.

"Yes, it was," says BJ in a slightly calmer voice. "I saw it too, Jess. You could've stopped if you wanted to. You just barreled right into her. Intentionally."

"You don't know that for a fact," says Jess.

"We're not blind, Jess!" yells Lauren. She's standing in front of her now, just inches from Jess's face. "We know what you're doing!"

"You've had it out for Ramie all day," says Kara Landrum, a senior who usually plays center.

"Yeah, everyone can see it," says another player.

"What's the problem?" asks Coach as he finally steps onto the court and walks toward us.

"The problem is that Jess is way outta control," says Lauren. "She's trying to *kill* Ramie."

"You okay, Grant?" Coach comes closer and peers down at me now.

I rub my right hand along my throbbing left arm. "I think I did something to my wrist."

"Help her up," he tells my teammates. Lauren and Kara carefully help me to my feet as I protect my left arm. "Let's see that." He examines my wrist, which is starting swell, and then nods. "Yep, looks like you may have busted something, Grant." He turns to Kara. "Get an icepack, will ya?"

"Oh no," moans Lauren. Then she points her forefinger at Jess. "This is your fault! If Ramie's arm is broken and she ends up missing the season, we'll all have you to thank, Jess!"

"Way to go, Jess," says someone else.

"There goes our chance for state," says Amy.

Without saying anything, Jess just walks off.

"Help Ramie over to the bleachers," Coach tells my friends.

"I can walk," I tell them as they hover like flies, guiding me to the bleachers, where they sit me down.

"Do you want me to call your parents?" asks Coach. "Or do you think you need paramedics?"

I kind of laugh. "No way am I going outta here in an ambulance. "Just call my mom, okay?" And then I tell him the number.

The coach tells the girls to continue the game while he makes the call. I watch from the sidelines, trying to focus on the players instead of the growing pain in my wrist. After about thirty minutes my mom shows up, looking worried and upset. She hurries over to me and I assure her that I'm okay, but that I probably need some medical attention.

"Jess was trying to take her out," Lauren tells my mom.

"Yeah," says Amy. "She looked like she wanted to kill her."

"Really?" My mom's brows raise with interest. "Why would Jess do that?"

Some of the girls kind of laugh now, and some even make some crude comments about Jess's messed-up mind, and all I want is to get out of here. "Let's go, Mom," I tell her as I stand.

"Well, Jess has always been a good friend to Ramie," Mom says as we're leaving. "I'm sure that whatever happened was purely accidental."

"Yeah, right," says Amy with a snort.

Coach offers to bring my bike home for me in his pickup, and I tell BJ where the key to my bike lock is.

"And I'll get your stuff for you," says BJ.

"Thanks."

When Mom and I are outside, I actually start feeling a little unsteady on my feet, like the ground isn't quite even or maybe it's moving. "Can I hold on to you?" I ask.

"Of course. Are you sure you're okay?" She looks at me with concern.

"I hit my head when I fell," I admit. "I guess I'm kinda dizzy.

So Mom helps me into the car and even gives me a blanket to wrap up in, since I'm still just wearing my jersey and shorts, which are pretty sweaty and cold. It's comforting to see her taking care of me like this, but at the same time I'm worried. What if my wrist really is broken? What if I really am out for the season? I felt like I was going bonkers after missing just one day of practice last week. How will I handle a whole season of sitting on the sidelines?

Was this really Jess's fault? Did she really hit me like that on purpose? Thinking back, it did seem like it was a full-impact collision, with no holding back. But then Jess, although shorter than me, probably outweighs me by fifty pounds. She could easily knock me over without trying too hard. Still, I have to admit that the hit felt like more than just an accident. It felt like she really did want to take me out. Why does she hate me so much?

thirteen

AFTER WHAT SEEMS TO TAKE FOREVER TO BE EXAMINED AND X-RAYED AND examined again, my wrist turns out to be moderately sprained, which means that although some ligaments have been torn, none have completely detached from the bone. This is good news.

The doctor prescribes the RICE treatment, which means (1) Rest for forty-eight hours, (2) Ice packs every twenty minutes, (3) Compression via an elastic wrap, and (4) Elevation above my heart.

"Does this mean I can't go out tonight?" I ask the doctor.

She laughs. "Yes, I'm afraid so. Between your wrist injury and the blow to your head, you need to remain quiet and just rest tonight and tomorrow too."

"What about basketball?" I ask her. "Do you think I'll be able to play this season?"

"I doubt that you'll be playing for at least a week or two," she says as she wraps my wrist. "But, like I told your mom, you need to schedule an appointment with your own family doctor or a sports physician next week. He or she can give you a more accurate prognosis."

As we wait for someone to return with my prescription for pain meds and some release papers, Mom helps me to dial Mitch's number on my cell phone. I'm guessing he's at work, since he doesn't answer, but I leave a message anyway, explaining the situation, and then Mom hangs up for me.

I know it's silly, but I can tell I'm close to tears. Why is this happening to me?

"Sorry, honey," she tells me. "But I'm sure Mitch will understand."

Finally, we're back at home. I am so tired I'm not sure I can make it up the steps to my room, but maybe it's the pain medication.

"Why don't you stay down here on the couch," Mom suggests. "That way I can hear you better if you need something."

So she brings me a pillow and a fluffy comforter, and soon I am settled in the family room. I'm surprised at how kind and caring my mom can be as she brings me things to eat and keeps changing my ice pack. It's not that my mom isn't normally a good mom, but I've never considered her a very nurturing person. Of course, that might be because Mom has always worked and I've always had a strong independent streak. Maybe I just never gave her the chance before.

Mom makes me turn my cell phone over to her, and then she fields a few calls for me. I can hear her explaining my condition and that I need to rest, but I can't tell who she's talking to. Finally, I decide that I don't really care and I just let myself drift off to sleep. I can't believe how tired I am.

I sleep off and on into Sunday, then I start to get antsy. So Mom helps me wrap my wrist in a plastic garbage bag and I manage to take a shower and put on some clean clothes.

"Did Mitch call today?" I ask Mom. I know that he called last night, and that she told him about my little accident. But he told her he'd call me today.

"No," she tells me.

"Oh."

"But Jess did."

I make a face.

"She told me she was sorry and that it was an accident, Ramie."

"What did you expect her to say? That she did it on purpose?"

"She wanted you to call her back."

"Yeah, right. Like that's going to happen."

Mom looks surprised. "You're not going to call her back?"

I scowl at her. "No, I'm not. Why should I?"

"Jess used to be your best friend, Ramie. You can't just wipe her out of your life because she's gay. She's still a person with feelings."

"Yeah, some pretty hateful feelings. You don't know what that felt like yesterday, Mom. She had it out for me during the whole practice. Everyone saw it. And when she hit me, it's like she really did want to kill me."

Mom shrugs. "Well, I suppose it's natural for her to feel some animosity toward you, Ramie."

"Why? I haven't done anything to her."

"Yes, that's the point. You *haven't* done anything. You avoid her, you don't return her calls, you're probably ignoring her at school, and I'm sure it's hurting her a lot."

"Hey, I'm the one in pain here," I remind her as I hold up my bandaged wrist.

"Your pain is only temporary."

"But Jess chose her pain, Mom. She brought it on herself. It wasn't my fault."

Mom just gives me that look now, the one that suggests I don't really understand this whole thing. And so I give the look right back to her, plus a little more.

"You may be a family counselor, Mom," I say, "But you don't know squat about some things." Then I march up to my room and slam my door. Okay, immature, I know. But how can my mom be so dense?

It's about five when Mitch calls me on my cell phone and asks if it's okay to come see me.

"It's way better than okay," I tell him. "I was just wondering if it's possible to die from boredom."

"I just got off work and thought I'd pick up something to eat. Can I bring you something too?"

"Sure."

"Pizza sound okay?"

"Pizza is perfect."

Then I hang up and call down to Mom, telling her not to fix me any dinner, since Mitch is bringing pizza.

"Then maybe you won't mind if I go to the gym with Brenda," she says.

"Fine with me," I tell her. Actually, it's fantastic with me. I mean I do appreciate her help this weekend, but I think we've both maxed out our limit on mother-daughter bonding time.

I spend a little time primping before I go downstairs to make sure the house is presentable, which it is, and before long Mitch shows up.

"That smells yummy," I say as I lead him into the kitchen. "Just what the doctor ordered."

He sets the box on the island, then leans over and gives me a gentle kiss on the cheek. "That looks like it hurt." He points to the lump in the middle of my forehead.

"Yeah." I open the lid and peak into the box. "But not as much as my wrist."

"How did it happen anyway?" He removes his jacket, then hangs it on the back of the bar stool.

"My mom didn't tell you?"

"No. She just said it was a basketball injury."

I kind of laugh as I use my good hand to reach for plates.

"Here, let me help," he offers, reaching over my shoulder to get them for me.

Soon we're both sitting at the island and, as we eat, I tell him the story of how Jess tackled me during the scrimmage.

"You're kidding?"

"I wish."

"She really did it on purpose?"

"That's what everyone said. She'd been playing pretty rough before that. I mean if it had been a real game, I'm sure she would've been out of there." I take another piece of pizza. "I never even saw her coming, but when she hit me, I went flying."

"Man, if she was a guy, I'd let her have it." Then he chuckles. "On second thought, maybe she sort of is a guy."

I make a face. "That's not funny."

"What did the coach say?"

I roll my eyes. "Not much. He has a don't-ask-don't-tell policy and says we girls have to sort these things out among ourselves, thank you very much."

"So, it's okay if Jess kills you then?"

"I guess."

"That's messed up, Ramie."

"I know."

"Are you out for the season?"

"I don't know."

"Do you care?"

I set down my drink. "Actually, I do care. I decided to go back and I really do want to play. But this whole thing with Jess kinda puts a damper on things. I just told myself to ignore her and to do my best, and then this happens." I hold up my wrist and just shake my head.

"Someone ought to set that girl straight," he says.

I laugh. "Was that a pun?"

"Maybe."

"I wish she would go back to straight."

"Well, that's probably not going to happen, Ramie. You might as well accept that Jess is a lesbian and just move on. Just get over it, you know."

"That's easier said than done."

He nods. "Yeah, I'm sure it is. If it makes you feel any better, even my dad is a little stumped about this whole thing."

"So, he knows about Jess?"

"Yeah. I heard him and my mom talking. Jess's mom and my mom are pretty good friends, you know. Mrs. LeCroix told my mom the whole story."

"So, what does your dad plan to do?"

"He said he's praying about it."

Just then the doorbell rings. "I wonder who that is," I say, starting to get up.

"Why don't you let me get it?" he offers.

The next thing I know Jess is standing in my house and both Mitch and I are kind of speechless. Like, speak of the devil. Not that Jess is the devil exactly. But, still, it's pretty weird seeing her here, especially after we were just talking about her.

"You didn't return my call," she says, looking down at the floor.

"Sorry," I say in a halfhearted way. "I was kind of knocked out by the pain pills."

She glances over at Mitch and then back at me. "Yeah, I can see that."

I stare at her. Now what is *that* supposed to mean?

"Anyway," she continues, "I wanted to come tell you that I'm sorry. I told your mom yesterday, but I thought I should tell you too, in person, you know."

"Oh."

"I didn't mean to hurt you."

I take a step closer to her now. She's barely in the living room, but I'm clean over on the other side. Mitch is about halfway between us, leaning against the couch and watching.

"You didn't mean to hurt me?" I repeat as I slowly walk toward her.

"It was an accident."

I just shake my head. "Wow, that was some accident, Jess."

"I didn't do it on purpose!"

"Fine," I say in an irritated voice, holding up my bandaged left wrist as if it's a visual aid. "Whatever."

"I *didn't!*"

"Then why did you come here?" I ask. "Why are you telling me that you're sorry?"

"Because I'm sorry you got hurt."

"Oh, but it's not your fault?"

"I *told* you, I *didn't* mean to do it!"

"Hey, I never said you did," I say in a quiet but cynical tone. I'm getting mad now. Why did she come here to say she's sorry if she's not? Why does she seem so intent on torturing me like this? Why can't she just leave me alone? I want to scream!

"You might as well say it, Ramie. Everyone else is saying it!"

"I can't control what everyone else is saying, Jess."

"Maybe not, but you don't have to add fuel to their fire."

"*What?*" I stare at her as if she's a stranger. Once again, I'm trying

119

to remember why we were ever friends in the first place. How could I stand being around her all those years? Was I really that desperate?

"You *know* what you're doing, Ramie. Oh sure, you pretend to be this strong and caring Christian, but you're just a phony—a big hypocrite. You're turning everyone against me, and you know it."

"You are totally crazy, Jess!" I glance over at Mitch now, hoping that maybe he can jump in and say something to help, but he seems just as bewildered as I am.

"Thanks." She tosses us both a plastic smile. "That's just the kind of affirmation I was looking for tonight. Thanks for caring, both of you."

"Why am I always the bad guy with you?" I demand. "Like you pretend to come over here to apologize to me tonight, but then you end up pointing the finger at me again. Like your problems are all my fault, Jess. I don't get you. It's like you want to blame me for everything."

"I'm not blaming you for everything. But, hey, if the shoe fits, wear it."

"What is that supposed to mean?" I demand.

"It means that you are not totally innocent, Ramie. You can't keep playing the poor little victim all the time. And you can't keep casting me as the evil and twisted friend who is ruining your life."

"What are you talking about?"

"The way you go around acting like *poor Ramie*, like this is all about you, like you're the only one who's hurting here. Well, here's a news bulletin: I'm hurting too!"

I nod as I walk closer. "Yeah, I can see you're hurting, Jess. I can see that you're totally miserable. But it's your fault. You brought this on yourself." I turn and look at Mitch. "I don't know why they call it *gay*," I say to him. "It sure doesn't look like it's making her happy!"

Jess takes a step toward me now, and we're only a few feet apart. Her eyes are narrowed in anger and her hands are curled into tight fists. It looks like she wants to hit me, like she wants to finish what she started, and suddenly I feel seriously scared. "You're the one who's making me miserable!" she yells. "You're the one who seems set on destroying my life!"

"Okay," says Mitch, stepping between us, his back to me. "Calm down, Jess. Getting upset is not going to help—"

"Don't tell me to calm down!" she yells.

"If you can't calm down, I think you should leave," he says in a very grown-up voice that makes me appreciate him even more.

"This is between Ramie and me, Mitch! It's none of your stinking business!"

"Ramie is *my* girlfriend," he tells her. "So that makes this my business. And I can understand how that might make you jealous, but you're going to have to get over it because Ramie is not a lesbian and she never will be."

Okay, I'm kind of shocked by this. But at the same time I'm relieved. I'm glad he said it. It's something I've wanted to say myself but just couldn't put into words. Then Jess does something I've never heard her do before. She uses some bad language. She cusses at both of us. Then she turns around and storms out, slamming the front door so loud that one of my mom's glass figurines falls out of the window and crashes onto the slate floor.

I'm shaking as I lean into Mitch. "Thank you," I tell him.

He runs his hand over my hair. "What a witch," he says. "It's hard to believe you guys were ever friends."

"She's changed, Mitch." I press my head into his shoulder as tears begin to pour down. "She's really changed."

fourteen

My doctor gives me the okay to go to practice during the next week, but only to stay in shape, and I must wear a wrist splint. He makes me promise that I won't do anything that might stress my wrist. No scrimmages, no passing drills, and no direct contact. Mostly I just dribble and jog and try to shoot with one hand. Then I sit in the bleachers and watch as the others play, or else I do my homework. It's better than nothing. I also keep stats for our first preseason game, which we lose. And then I go back to my doctor the following week, telling him that I think my wrist is almost well, but he's not convinced.

"You can keep going to practice," he says. "But no actual games until the real season begins. Isn't that after Christmas anyway?"

"Yeah," I admit with disappointment. "But we have Rendezvous next weekend. It's an invitational tournament, and everyone was hoping I'd be able to play."

"Sorry." He frowns as he closes the chart. "The last thing you need is to play a bunch of games all in one day, Ramona."

I know he's probably right, but everyone on the team is really disappointed. Well, everyone but Jess. I'm sure she's elated. But she and I do not speak. We keep a good distance between us. And we don't even make eye contact. Sometimes I imagine that she doesn't even exist, or that I don't know her, and that I never did.

Frankly, I'm surprised that she hasn't quit the team. Everyone treats her like she's carrying some dreaded disease. But then she loves basketball. I guess she loves it enough to put up with the crud that girls toss at her. And I have to admit that I don't mind when they do. Of course, I don't say any of that stuff myself. I know it's not Christlike. But I don't defend her either, even though I know that too isn't Christlike. Jess has obviously found a different place to get dressed down. We never see her in the girls' locker room anymore. I'm guessing she uses a stall in the restroom, since I saw her coming out of there once with her gym bag, completely dressed. And she probably showers at home. I know it must be inconvenient, but it's an inconvenience she has brought on herself. I don't see any reason she should make the rest of us suffer.

Rendezvous is on the first Saturday of Christmas break. It's a two-hour bus ride to Arrington, but we make the most of it with lots of junk food and card games and craziness. BJ brought her CD player, and we even take turns dancing in the aisle. It's like a party on wheels. Somehow Coach Ackley manages to sleep up front. And clear in the back, all by herself, Jess appears to be sleeping too. However, I know it's just an act. For one thing, Jess is such a light sleeper that our noise would keep her awake, but besides that, she's never been able to sleep in a moving vehicle. What a faker.

Our team wins its first game and hopes rise, but then we lose the next one by just a few points, and then we're creamed in the third one, which puts us out of the tournament.

"We needed you out there today, Ramie," says BJ as we trudge back to the bus.

"Yeah," says Lauren. "I was wishing I knew some kind of magic trick so we could trade Jess for you."

This is followed by laughter, including mine. But I feel a twinge of guilt when I notice that Jess is within hearing distance. Still, she wasn't exactly having a good game today, and there were several times when the team's patience wore thin with her bad attitude. Toward the end of the second game, just when it looked like our team might've been making a comeback, Jess goes and gets us a technical foul. After that, team morale went right down the toilet.

"Maybe Jess should switch over to the guys' team," says Amy a little too loudly. "They could probably use a tough guy like her."

This time our laughter is interrupted by a loud, "Shut up!" followed by some off-color swear words.

"LeCroix!" barks Coach Ackley as he's walking up behind us with the ball bag hoisted over his shoulder. "Give me thirty!"

"Right here?" Jess stops in the freezing parking lot that we're crossing.

"Hit the pavement! *Now!*"

Jess drops to the icy ground in pushup mode, and Coach continues walking toward the bus. Meanwhile, the rest of us stand around her in a semicircle, staring as Jess begins doing her mandatory pushups. She still has on her sweaty uniform, whereas the rest of us have all showered and changed into regular clothes. Her dark curly hair is matted down and sticking to her forehead, and her face is blotchy and red as she huffs her way up and down, up and down. Lauren is counting for her, but then a girl from the JV team joins her, saying, "Seven *butch* pushups, eight *butch* pushups . . ."

Soon others chime in and everyone is counting "*butch* pushups" as if it's the funniest thing ever.

"Stupid homo," says another girl.

"It's jock-chicks like her that make us all look bad."

Some crueler and even more vulgar comments are tossed out, and finally, feeling ashamed for all of us, I go back to the bus.

Coach Ackley's nose is stuck in *Sports Illustrated*, and he merely grunts as I walk past him. The JV coach has her eyes closed as she listens to her MP3 player, just basically checked out.

I go back through the bus about midway and sit down, watching the circle of girls through the window. The way they're clustered around Jess reminds me of the kind of mob that gathers when a fight erupts, with bloodthirsty kids watching and egging the fighters on for their own selfish entertainment. And then it hits me. The scene out there reminds me of something else too, something I'm not willing to face or even acknowledge just now.

Pushing unwanted images from my head, I try to grasp that it's Jess who is at the center of this mob, and I try to remember exactly why and how this happened. Didn't she bring this on herself by using bad language? I find it hard to believe that this person on the ground, the foulmouthed lesbian girl who is being humiliated and teased, is really my old best friend. How can that be?

I can't take it anymore. I just look away. They all make me sick. Jess makes me sick. This whole stinking world makes me sick. I close my eyes and wish it would all go away.

Now they are piling back onto the bus. Gay and butch jokes are still being tossed about, but not quite as loudly. Not that it matters, since both the varsity and the JV coach appear to be totally tuned out anyway. I try not to look up as Jess comes in the door. But I can see that her face is even redder than before. She doesn't say a word as she makes her way down the crowded aisle amid the quiet but jagged taunts. I keep my eyes down as she huffs past me, her gym bag brushing against my shoulder. BJ, directly behind her, stops at my row and looks at me. I scoot over and she takes the empty seat beside me. Then BJ slumps down, folds her arms across her chest, and lets out what sounds like a very frustrated sigh.

"What?" I whisper.

"I am so sick of this."

I nod. "Yeah. You and me both."

"What are we going to do?"

I turn and stare at her. "What do you mean? What *can* we do?"

"It's wrong to just sit by and watch them treating her like that."

"But really, what can we do?" Okay, I'm actually wondering why we should do anything. Isn't this just one of those natural-consequence scenarios my mom is always talking about? Jess comes out of her closet and some people don't like it.

"What do you think Jesus would do?"

I turn toward the foggy window. Wiping a clean patch on the glass, I stare out at the parking lot, watching as the last of the girls trickle onto the bus. It's not even four o'clock, but it's getting dusky already. The driver closes the door, checks with the coaches, and the bus takes off.

"Ramie?"

I keep looking out the window.

"We need to stand by Jess."

Then I turn around and give BJ the blankest of blank looks, like I totally don't get what she's saying.

"You know that we have to stand by her."

"I don't *know* that, BJ."

"You know that's what Jesus would do."

I frown at her. "So you're saying that we should endorse homosexuality? Should we stand up and say that gay's okay?"

"I'm not saying we should condone it, Ramie."

"But if we stand by Jess, isn't that the same as condoning it?"

"No. I don't think it is."

"Well what about you, just now?" I challenge her. "You stayed out there with everyone else. You stood with the others who were teasing Jess and calling her sleazy names. Is that what Jesus would do, BJ?" Okay, I think I've got her on the defense now. This should shut her up.

"For your information, Ramie, I stayed out there to make sure that no one hurt Jess. They were getting pretty rowdy and I was ready to protect her if anyone got too carried away."

"Oh."

"Okay, I know this is hard for you, Ramie. Jess was your best friend and her little announcement puts you in a tough spot. But, as a Christian, don't you see that we can't let this continue? Seriously, you should've heard them out there. It would've been so easy for it to get out of hand. And what then?"

"I don't know."

"Well, I'm fed up." Now BJ stands.

"What are you doing?"

"I'm going to sit with Jess."

I just stare at her. How can she do this? Why?

"Are you coming with me?"

I turn and look away.

"Fine."

When I look back, BJ is gone. I am sitting by myself, and this time I'm the one who's pretending to be asleep. But I'm really just thinking. Thinking and praying. For the first time since this whole nightmare began, I'm trying to get honest with myself. Honest with myself and with God. I replay those uncomfortable images of the mob that surrounded Jess out on the parking lot. Only this time, I allow myself to admit that the scene reminded me of something from the Bible. It reminded me of the time when the religious leaders threw the woman who'd been caught in adultery at Jesus' feet. I remember how they wanted Jesus to condemn the sinful woman so that they could stone her. And it reminded me of how Jesus said those famous words, "If any one of you is without sin, let him be the first to throw a stone at her."

And that just nails me. I realize that I am the one who threw the first stone into Jess's life. Oh, not literally. But I was the first one that Jess confided in and, as a result, I was the first one to judge her, to condemn her . . . to basically hate her.

I am ashamed. Really ashamed.

I keep on praying. I confess my sins to God, and I ask him to forgive me. But eventually I realize that I will have to do more than just bring this to God. In fact, I have no doubt about what I need to do. And as hard as it might be to do this thing, I know that my life will only get harder if I don't. I also know that I can't put it off for one more day, or one more hour, or even one more minute.

God help me, please, please, help me.

fifteen

IT TAKES A REAL ACT OF MY WILL TO PEEL MYSELF OFF OF THE SEAT AND HEAD to the back of the bus. Most of the girls have quieted down now. Some are listening to MP3 players and a lot of them are asleep. But in the dim light I can see BJ and Jess, sitting in the backseat, and it looks like they're talking. But when they see me coming their way, they stop. I can feel both pairs of eyes on me, and I'm not sure that I'm actually welcome back here. But as I get closer, I can see that Jess has been crying. She quickly wipes her cheeks and, as she looks away, I can tell she's embarrassed. She doesn't want me to see her like this.

I hold my hands up, almost as if I've come to surrender. "I know you probably don't want to talk to me, Jess. And I understand. But I need to tell you that God has just convicted me."

She looks at me. I can't tell if she's curious or skeptical. But I know I have her attention.

"Just now, God showed me that I need to come and apologize to you. I need to tell you that I'm sorry for judging you. And I'm sorry for being mean to you. And I need to ask you to forgive me." I wait for her to respond.

She looks pretty stunned, but she just nods like she understands, like she's willing to forgive me. Then she starts crying again.

I look at BJ, unsure of what to do next. "Should I leave?" I ask her.

"No," says BJ. "Why don't you sit with us, Ramie?"

So I sit down beside BJ. Jess is sitting on the other side. I turn and face Jess, who looks totally miserable, and I wonder whether my confession is helping or hurting. But I honestly want her to know that I mean it.

"I really am sorry," I tell Jess again. "I mean I still don't understand this whole thing with you. And I still have questions and concerns, but I am so sorry for treating you the way I did."

Jess looks across BJ with tears still streaming down her face. "I'm sorry too, Ramie. I treated you bad too. Probably even worse than you did me."

I shrug. "I don't know."

"Yeah, well, I really am sorry." She points to my wrist now. "And even though I kept telling myself that was an accident . . . well, I don't really know for sure that it was. It's like it just happened and I don't even know how exactly. But I was really angry that day. And maybe it was one of those Freudian things, where I meant to do it on some subconscious level."

"Well, I forgive you," I tell her.

BJ looks at Jess now. "Have you ever told Ramie what you just told me?"

Jess shakes her head and looks down at her lap.

"What?" I ask.

"Jess would have to tell you," says BJ. "I mean if she wants to. But I think you should hear it."

"She might not want to hear it," Jess says sadly.

"She needs to hear it, Jess."

"It's okay," I assure her, preparing myself for the worst. "Whatever it is, I do want to hear it."

"It's something that happened a while back," Jess begins. "The summer when I was twelve. It happened at soccer camp, that year when you got strep throat and couldn't go to camp. Remember?"

"Yeah. I was so bummed."

"You should've been glad." Then Jess goes on to tell about how one of the college-aged soccer coaches was really friendly to her. "Her name was Ashley Farrell, and she was our cabin leader."

"Oh yeah," I tell her. "I remember how you wrote a couple of letters from camp, and you went on and on about how cool this Ashley chick was. You said she was really helping you with your game. I was so jealous."

"You shouldn't have been." Then Jess tells me about how Ashley would ask Jess to give her back rubs at night. "It didn't seem like a big deal," she says. "And afterward Ashley would insist on rubbing my back in return . . . and then it just kept on going."

"Kept on going?" I query, unsure that I really want to hear this, but knowing that I probably need to, and Jess probably needs to tell me. Even so, I'm starting to feel slightly sick. I take in a deep breath.

Then Jess puts her head down between her knees. "This is so hard, Ramie."

"Go ahead," BJ encourages her. "Get it out."

Jess sits up now. "After everyone in the cabin was asleep, Ashley would come and get in bed with me. And she would do things, you know, things I'd never had anyone do to me before. And she would tell me that she loved me and that it was okay and that I was her favorite camper and the best soccer player and stuff like that." And then Jess begins to cry again. "And when I told her I didn't want her to do it anymore, she got mad. Then she made me promise not to tell anyone, saying that we'd both get into trouble and get kicked out of camp and my parents would find out and all kinds of horrible stuff. So I didn't make her stop."

"She sexually abused you?" I whisper, worried that someone else might be listening, although the seats ahead of us are empty and the rumbling noise from the bus's engine seems to be pretty good sound camouflage.

Jess shrugs. "I didn't make her stop."

"She was a grown-up, Jess. You were a kid. That's called sexual abuse," says BJ in a very authoritative tone.

"BJ's right," I agree, trying to imagine how it would feel to be hurt like that, to have someone you liked and trusted take advantage of you in such a creepy way. "You were sexually abused at soccer camp, Jess."

"But it was my fault too," Jess says, looking down. "It made me uncomfortable and I was ashamed, but I never made her stop. It's like I wanted to believe everything she said to me, all the good stuff, I mean. But at the same time I knew what we were doing was wrong."

"So you've lived with that for these past four years?" I ask.

She nods, then looks down, and I can tell she's ashamed.

"And that's why you think you're gay?"

I can't really read Jess's expression, but it seems to be a mixture of humiliation and anger. "I *am* gay, Ramie. I mean I probably would've figured it out sooner or later. But the thing is, part of me liked the way Ashley made me feel." She stares at me now. "I wouldn't have liked it if I wasn't gay."

I look at BJ now, feeling like I'm over my head.

"You need to talk to a counselor," BJ tells Jess.

I think of my mom. And I know exactly what kind of counsel my mom would give Jess. She would tell her that it's okay to be a lesbian and that she should join some kind of a homosexual support group where she can talk about her feelings, and she'd give her books on homosexuality to read and just basically condone her as a lesbian. Ugh.

"I agree that Jess needs to talk to someone," I say quickly. "But how about a Christian counselor?"

"So they can tell me that I'm sinning and condemn me?" Jess shoots back.

"No." I consider this. Then I tell Jess about the image that went through my head earlier, the image of Jesus and the woman caught in adultery. "He didn't condemn her, Jess. He forgave her. Then he told her to go and sin no more."

"But see, you're still saying that it's sinful to be homosexual. Not everyone agrees with you on that, Ramie. You should go to some of the meetings I've been to. You might begin to see things differently."

I hold up my hand so she can see I'm still wearing my promise ring, the one that her dad gave me, just like the one he gave to her. "Remember this?"

She nods, then looks down to her own hand, where I've already noticed the band of gold is missing from her finger.

"Well, I still believe in it, Jess. I still believe that sex outside of marriage is sin. Do you?"

"I don't know."

"Really?" I push her. "Tell the truth, Jess. Do you think it's okay now? Do you think that just because you've come out as a homosexual that the rules have all changed, and it's okay to have sex whenever you like now?"

"I'm not sure."

"Maybe Ramie's right, Jess," says BJ. "Maybe you should see

a Christian counselor. At least to start with. I mean you're still a Christian, aren't you?"

"I don't know. I mean I think I am. But I know I haven't been acting much like it lately."

"None of us have," I remind her.

"If it would help, we could go with you," offers BJ. "I guess I can't speak for Ramie. But I'd come with you, if you wanted some support."

"I would too," I say. "I mean if it would help."

"Who would I talk to?" asks Jess.

Our youth pastor immediately comes to mind. "How about Nathan? I mean he acts like a goofball sometimes, but he does have a degree in counseling."

Jess considers this. "Yeah. I guess Nathan seems pretty open-minded. For a Christian anyway. But just because I'm willing to talk to him doesn't mean I'm going to change my mind or anything."

"I know," I tell her. But I'm thinking maybe we're all changing. We talk some more and for the first time since Jess "came out," I'm beginning to see that my old friend still lives. But it seems like she's trapped in this persona, this lesbian image that she's been working so hard to create. It seems to surround her, almost like a protective shell.

Then the bus is pulling into the school parking lot, and everyone starts waking up and gathering their stuff, and it's getting noisy again. Then, of course, one of the girls looks back and notices the three of us still sitting in the back of the bus, and she makes this really raunchy comment. And everyone else just laughs.

I stand up now, and I am really, really mad. What right do they have to treat people like this? "I am so sick of you guys!" I yell this so loud that the whole bus immediately gets quiet. I march up the aisle now and then I look this girl right in the face. "And I swear if

Coach Ackley doesn't make you guys straighten up and stop this infantile nasty talk, then someone else will!" I glare at Coach. He has this mixture of surprise and amusement across his face. "I mean it!" I tell him, shaking my splinted wrist toward him. "Either you do something or I will go to Ms. Fremont and I will tell her exactly what's going on here."

He nods and actually seems somewhat pleased. "Yeah, I'm getting a little fed up with this too," he yells. "The next girl who gets out of line will be suspended from the team for one week. You got that?"

And maybe they do. Because as we exit the bus and head over to the parking lot, no one says anything off-color. But I can feel Lauren and Amy watching the three of us, since BJ and I are still walking with Jess. I can tell they're wondering what's up.

"You still need a ride, Ramie?" BJ asks me in a tired voice.

I glance over at Jess. "Well, unless Jess wants to give me ride."

"Sure, I can drop you," she says in an offhand way, but I can tell she's surprised.

"Okay." I wave good-bye to BJ.

"You guys better not forget we have practice next week," warns BJ.

"I know," I call back. "Even though it's Christmas break."

"No rest for the wicked," says Lauren as she and Amy join us. Even though the parking lot lights aren't the brightest, I can see the questioning looks these two are giving me as I follow Jess to her car. Like they want to ask what gives.

"See you guys next week," I say to Lauren and Amy in what I hope sounds like a positive tone, tossing them a reassuring smile. I want them to know that we're okay. At least I hope we are. But as I climb into Jess's car, I have to admit that I feel pretty nervous. I hope this isn't a mistake.

We're both really quiet at first. Part of me is ready for small talk, but at the same time I know that small talk won't work.

"So you're going out with Mitch?" Jess says as she pulls out of the parking lot.

"Yeah," I say. "Which reminds me—it's youth group tonight. Are you going?"

"Oh, I don't know."

"You haven't been there . . . well, you know . . . since you . . . *came out.*"

"Don't you hate those words? *Came out?* I mean it sounds almost like a disease. Like you *came* down with something. Or maybe you broke *out* with something. Or you put them together and you *came out.*"

That makes me laugh. Then Jess laughs.

"You know it's not that I've never been around homosexuals before," I tell her. "I mean my mom has some friends. And I've always just treated them like everyone else. But it just freaked me out when it was you, Jess. Can you understand that?"

"Yeah, it's pretty much freaked out everyone."

"How's your family doing?"

"Not so well. My mom tries to hide it, but I know she's really depressed. I've heard her crying a lot."

"Yeah, she seemed pretty sad the time I talked to her."

"She told my family about the exit group and they all think I should go." Jess lets out a groan. "Why does everyone have this pressing need to *fix* me?"

"I don't know. I guess it's because we just want you to be happy, Jess. And it's hard for some of us to believe that being gay is going to make you happy."

"When you say it like that—*being* gay—it's like you think it's something temporary, like an emotion. You're *being* moody. Or you're *being* funny. I really don't think it's a temporary thing, Ramie."

"But how do you know?"

"I know how I feel."

"You mean about girls?" I ask, knowing that I'm probably heading in a direction that I don't really want to go. Or maybe I do.

"You mean do I get excited about girls? Do I think girls are hot? Is that what you're asking me, Ramie?" I can hear anger in her voice now.

"Well, isn't that what being a lesbian is all about?"

"That's part of it. But it's not everything. It's not all about sex."

I want to say, "Yeah, right," but I control myself. "Well, what's it about then?"

"It's about how I feel *inside*. I've never been a girly-girl, Ramie. You know that. I've always liked boys' clothes and playing sports and—"

"Hey, that pretty much describes me too."

"No way," she says. "You *like* girly things, Ramie. You know you do."

"Well, I didn't always. I used to be a tomboy too. I think I just kind of grew into liking them."

"Well, I didn't."

"Maybe you just never gave yourself the chance, Jess. Maybe you're just afraid to let your feminine side out."

"Maybe I don't have a feminine side."

"I think you do. I just think you keep it well hidden."

"I think you just wish that was true, Ramie."

"Maybe I do. Maybe for your sake I do."

"See, you're just like my family. You want to fix me."

"I just want you to have the best life you can possibly have, Jess. And I want you to keep walking with God and obeying him."

"And you think I can't do that and be gay too?"

"I know some people think you can. My mom has made that perfectly clear to me. But I just don't think that's what the Bible says."

We're at my house now, and although I think some good things might have been said during the ride, I am so glad to be home.

"Look, Jess," I say as she waits for me to get out. "I know that this isn't going to be easy. I'm not even sure that I can handle having a lesbian friend. To be perfectly honest, it still creeps me out some. I mean I do care about you, and I don't want us to fight anymore. But I'm not sure how much I can really handle."

"Yeah, I figured as much."

"Hey, I'm just trying to be honest, Jess. I will do everything I can to be your friend, but this is still hard for me."

"You think it's easy for me?"

"I think we all need some really good counseling."

"Well, I'm willing to give Nathan a try. But if he jumps right into trying to fix me, I will be so outta there."

"That's understandable." I open the car door. "Thanks for the ride."

"Thanks for talking to me tonight."

"Well, I think it really helps me to understand you a little better. I mean I feel really bad about what happened to you at soccer camp and I—"

"But I don't want you guys to blame it on that, okay? I was just trying to make you see where I'm coming from, how I've known this for a long time. It's not just something I woke up and decided to do one morning. Sheesh, that's what my family thinks."

"You haven't told them about camp?"

"They are hardly talking to me at all, Ramie. I mostly just stay out of their way. Try not to keep rocking their boat. I wish I was a senior this year. Then I could just leave home and get on with my life."

"I have one last question, Jess. Do you mind?"

She rolls her eyes. "Yeah, go ahead. I already feel like I've been through the grinder tonight anyway."

"Well, are you like involved with another girl now? Is that what made you want to come out of the closet? I mean is there someone that you—"

"No, Ramie!" Then she laughs. "Why? Are you jealous?"

I make a face at her. "No. I was just curious."

"No. If it makes you feel any better, I've never been involved with another girl. Not since the thing with Ashley. But I'll admit that I've had impulses. Okay? Does that make you happy?"

I frown. "Why would that make me happy?"

"True confessions."

"So, have you ever had impulses . . . you know . . . toward me?" Okay, this question is really making me feel sick, but since I know I'm home and I can run into my house and get away from her if necessary, I'm willing to take the risk. Plus, I just really want to know.

"Yeah, I'm having an impulse right now, Ramie. I have this impulse to hit you." She makes a fist, then laughs. "No, I don't think I've really had an impulse toward you. I think I'd be more attracted to the real lesbian type, you know, the kind who might return the attraction."

I sigh and shake my head. "No, I don't really know. It's pretty hard to wrap my mind around that whole thing."

"Yeah, yeah. I know. We're all freaks."

"Well, thanks again for the ride." I get out of her car now. "And thanks for being honest with me."

"You too."

As I walk toward the house, I wonder if this is a relationship that can actually be maintained. I mean sure, we may have made some progress tonight, but the idea of ever being really close friends again, the possibility of sharing secrets, sleeping over, talking about boyfriends, shopping for bras . . . well, that seems to be something that's best left dead and buried.

That's sad, though, and I feel sorry for Jess. I mean who will she share those times with now? She can't do stuff like that with guys. And she can't do it with girls like me. What does that leave? Just lesbians like her? But that wouldn't be the same, would it? Wouldn't that be like me doing stuff like that with guys? Pretty weird. As I go into my house, I still feel confused. Very confused.

sixteen

I SUSPECT THAT I MIGHT BE THE MAIN REASON MITCH HAS BEEN CONSISTENTLY going to youth group these last few weeks. I still find his lacka-daisical approach rather ironic, since his dad is a pastor. But I'm beginning to accept that just because Mitch's parents are Christians doesn't necessarily mean that Mitch is saved. In fact, I'm beginning to understand that Mitch is really struggling with his faith. But I'm not sure how I feel about that. I guess I'm thinking that as long as we go to youth group together and things don't get too out of hand in our relationship, we should be okay. At least for now.

Because for now, I still feel the need to be linked with a boyfriend. Okay, maybe I'm a little insecure about my sexual identity, which I know is silly, but if I'm going to try to have any kind of a friendship with Jess, I really want someone like Mitch around. I just don't want people assuming that I'm gay, or that I'm not the kind of Christian I claim to be.

I'm not surprised when Jess doesn't show up at youth group tonight. But I hope that will be changing soon. And after youth group ends, I tell Mitch that I need to talk to Nathan.

His brows lift. "Is it something personal?"

I laugh. "No. I just want to ask him something about Jess. It has to do with what I already told you, about what happened on the bus today. You can come with me if you want." I didn't give Mitch all the details about Jess, only that BJ and I were trying to reach out to her, and that she seems open to help.

I wave to BJ, who's talking to a friend over on the other side of the room. I clued her in earlier about my plan to talk to Nathan tonight. Then the three of us approach Nathan.

"We want to talk to you about Jess LeCroix," I tell Nathan.

He nods. "It's about time."

"She's really struggling," I begin. "BJ and I had a long talk with her on the way home from Rendezvous."

"Hey, how'd you guys do?" he asks.

"Not so well," says BJ.

"Too bad. But tell me what's up with Jess?" he says. "I talked briefly with her parents last week. So I do know what's going on."

"Doesn't everyone?"

He smiles. "Yeah. Stuff like this pretty much rocks everyone's world. But it doesn't have to."

"Well, we were talking to Jess about getting some counseling," I say.

"Christian counseling," BJ adds.

"You mean you guys are going to try to talk her out of being gay?" says Mitch.

Nathan laughs. "You can't exactly talk someone out of that."

"I know," I add. "That's not it, really. We just think she needs to talk to someone about what's gone on with her. And she's kind of reluctant. So BJ and I offered to come with her, if you think that's a good idea."

He considers this. "Well, in this situation, that might be a good idea. At least for starters. Jess's hardest challenge, right now, might be her need for acceptance."

"Acceptance?" I echo. "As in accepting that she's gay?"

"Accepting her for who she is," he says. "Loving her unconditionally."

We talk a little more, and I can tell that Nathan is trying to make sure that BJ and I are really on the same page he is, and finally he invites the three of us girls to meet him for coffee next week.

"I think doing coffee is a little less intimidating than sitting in a counselor's office. It sets the stage for acceptance better."

So it's agreed. We'll meet him at Starbucks on Tuesday afternoon, following basketball practice.

"As long as Jess is still agreeable," I say finally.

"Let's all be praying for her," says Nathan. "Pray that she won't be on the defensive, that she'll feel our unconditional love." He glances over at Mitch now. "You coming too, bro?"

Mitch shrugs. "Maybe not. I wouldn't want to make her uncomfortable."

Nathan nods. "That's cool."

As Mitch drives me home, we talk a little more about Jess. But some of his questions bother me a little. And I get the feeling that he doesn't really care about her. Maybe even that he dislikes her. And that bugs me.

"I think you guys are wasting your time," he says finally. "I mean she's a lesbo, Ramie."

"Don't call her that."

"Okay. Sorry. She's a *lesbian*. Is that more politically correct? But, seriously, isn't it obvious?"

"What do you mean?"

"I mean I probably knew she was gay even before you did."

"How?"

"Just look at her, Ramie. She walks like a guy. She dresses like a guy. She's just your typical butch lesbian. I'm surprised you never figured it out before." He laughs. "Or did you?"

The way he asks that last question really makes me mad. "What's that supposed to mean?" I demand.

"Well, you know. Did she ever come on to you?"

"Mitch!"

"You're a hot girl, Ramie. I'm sure that Jess was aware of it. Are you saying that she never came on to you?"

Now I know he thinks he's being funny. And maybe I would've laughed at that before. Before I heard part of Jess's story today. But now it just sounds rude and crude and mean. And so I tell him.

"Wow, you're being pretty sensitive about this, Ramie," he says as he pulls into my driveway. "Sure I didn't touch a nerve?"

"No!" I snap at him. "Didn't you listen to anything that Nathan said tonight?"

"About what?"

"About loving Jess unconditionally."

"Who says I'm not?"

"You don't sound very loving to me."

"Hey, I'm the one who's accepting that she's gay. I'd say that's pretty unconditional."

"But what if she's not gay? What if she's just trapped?"

He laughs. "Yeah, right."

I let out an exasperated sigh, then open the door. But when Mitch walks me up the stairs to the door, I'm not feeling quite the same anticipation as usual. And instead of our regular little kissing session, which has been getting longer and longer, I let him kiss me once, then I quickly say good night and go into the house.

My mom is sitting at the island in the kitchen, working on her laptop. "How was youth group?" she asks.

"Okay." I open the fridge and look around.

"How was Mitch?"

I make a growling sound as I take out a can of soda.

She looks up from her computer screen. "Now was that a happy growl or a grumpy growl?"

"A grumpy one." I pop open the soda and take a sip.

Then she closes her laptop and looks at me. "What's wrong with Mitch?"

I pull out a stool and sit down across from her, considering how much I want to disclose. On one hand, if I tell her that Mitch thinks that Jess is hopeless and will always be gay, she'll probably agree. On the other hand, if I tell her that Mitch made some unkind remarks about Jess and me, she will probably think he's a jerk. So I decide to bring up something else.

"Can I tell you something protected by client confidentiality?" I ask.

"About yourself?"

"No, about someone else."

"Is this a real someone else, or is it you pretending to be someone else so that you can hear what I'd think?"

I roll my eyes. "No, it's really someone else, Mom."

She nods. "Yes. I can promise you client confidentiality."

"Okay. The someone else is Jess. I wouldn't have told you, but I figured you'd guess anyway."

"And?"

So I repeat what Jess told BJ and me on the bus. I repeat it with full details, and even as I retell Jess's story, I am hit again by the sadness of the situation. The unfairness of it.

Mom nods with a concerned expression. "Well, that casts this in a whole different light, doesn't it?"

"So, you're a professional," I say. "Do you think that Jess has assumed she's a lesbian just because of what that stupid Ashley did to her?"

"Being sexually abused as a child definitely impacts a person's identity, Ramie. Although I've read some research that doesn't statistically support what you're suggesting."

"But I've heard you say that research is subjective," I remind her.

She smiles. "You actually listen to me sometimes?"

Ignoring this, I plod on ahead. "So, it's possible that some research could be different? Like some research might prove that kids who get sexually abused by a same-sex person might believe that they're homosexual?"

"I'm sure it's possible."

"So maybe Jess really isn't gay," I say hopefully. "Maybe she's just been so affected by the abuse that she thinks she's gay."

"It's not as simple as that, Ramie."

"Why?"

"Well, you'd have to be Jess to know the answer to that question."

"But it's possible?"

"Anything is possible."

"But, Mom," I plead, "Doesn't it make sense? Doesn't it seem like Jess wouldn't have those feelings if Ashley hadn't messed with her? I mean Jess said it made her feel guilty and dirty and ashamed. Why would she feel like that if it was *normal?*"

"Because it was sexual abuse, Ramie. Jess would've felt just the same if a man had done it."

I feel ridiculous for failing to see that myself.

"But you are right about one thing."

"What?"

"Being sexually abused would mess up Jess's head." Mom gets a thoughtful look now. "And didn't Jess start putting on the weight about that same time? Wasn't she around twelve or thirteen when she started getting heavy?"

I think about this. "Yeah, now that you mention it, she never really was overweight before. Do you think that has something to do with it?"

"I think it's just symptomatic of how she felt about her body. Lots of sex-abuse victims will turn to things like food to compensate for their pain. It can take the form of overeating or even anorexia. Others might turn to drugs or alcohol. It's a coping mechanism. But counseling is better."

"But until today she never told anyone," I point out. "She's never had any counseling at all."

"It's not too late to get some."

So I tell Mom about our plan to meet with Nathan next week.

She nods. "That's a good start. But it may take more than that. It probably wouldn't hurt for her to be in a therapy group too."

I'm worried that Mom means a homosexual therapy group, and I know that Jess has already attended some gay alliance meetings with other homosexuals. I figure things like that will only push her the wrong way. But I don't say this.

"If Jess ever wants to talk to me," Mom offers, "I'd be more than happy."

"Yeah," I say. "I'll let her know." I probably won't let her know. Or, if I do, I won't encourage it. My mom means well, but until she understands that homosexuality is a moral issue, I just don't see how she could be much help to Jess.

"I'm glad that you're talking to her again, Ramie," Mom says. "I'm sure she needs her friends more than ever right now."

"Yeah. I feel bad that I was pushing her away," I confess. "It just made me so uncomfortable. I'm still a little worried everyone will think I'm a lesbian too." Then I tell her a little about what's been going on with the girls on the basketball team and even how I stood up to them today.

Mom smiles. "You did that, Ramie?"

I nod. "I think Coach Ackley was pretty shocked. But at least he supported me in it."

"He better support you! The school could end up with a nasty lawsuit on its hands if he doesn't. This is serious stuff these days, Ramie. Discrimination based on sexual orientation can get groups like the ACLU pretty riled up."

"Well, it got me pretty riled up to hear girls calling Jess all those names today." I don't tell her that Mitch made me almost as mad tonight when he said what I thought were some totally unkind words about Jess as well.

I still don't understand why he's taking such a strong position against her. Okay, maybe he actually thinks he's being supportive of Jess, but I just don't see it like that. Frankly, it almost seems like he's trying to drive an even bigger wedge between Jess and me. But why?

seventeen

"I can't give you a ride to practice today," Jess tells me on the phone just minutes before she is supposed to pick me up. But her voice sounds funny and I can tell something's not right.

"What's wrong?" I ask.

"I'm at the hospital."

"Are you okay?"

"Yeah. It's not me."

"What then?" I'm feeling really worried now. "Is it your dad?" I know her dad's been taking heart medicine. And all this stress about Jess can't be helping.

"No, it's not Dad. It's Joey."

"Joey?"

"Joey Pinckney."

"Joey Pinckney?" Now this makes no sense. Why is Jess at the hospital with Joey Pinckney?

"He tried to kill himself."

"Oh no! Is he okay?"

"We don't know. Some of us, you know, from the gay alliance group at school, we're here to support him."

"Oh."

"So I'm going to miss practice."

"That's understandable. I'll tell Coach. I just hope Joey is okay."

"Yeah, I'm sure you do." But something about the way she says this doesn't sound right. There's a sarcastic edge to it.

"I do, Jess. I like Joey."

"I'm sure that's why you tease him sometimes."

"Hey, I only teased him because I liked him. He was always cool with it before. If I didn't like him, I would've just ignored him. And lately, well, after I started to wonder about some things . . . well, I quit teasing him altogether."

"That probably didn't help."

"So this is *my* fault?" I say with indignation. "Joey tried to kill himself because of me?"

"Not you personally, Ramie. Just people like you."

"People like me?" I can hear my voice getting louder. "But we've been talking, Jess. We're working stuff out. Why are you saying this?"

"Because you have an agenda. People like you always do. You and BJ just want to see if you can fix me. Just like my parents. And it's people like you who make people like Joey want to kill themselves. I have to go now."

"Right."

"By the way, I won't be able to meet you guys with Nathan today." Then, before I can respond, she hangs up.

I call BJ's cell phone, knowing that she's probably already on her way to school.

"Jess can't come get me for practice," I tell her in an angry voice. "Tell Coach that I'm not going to make it either, okay?"

"Wait a minute, Ramie. What's wrong? What about our meeting with Nathan?"

So I fill her in about Joey, as well as Jess's new attitude toward us.

"It's like she's blaming us," I say. "Like we're personally responsible for Joey's suicide attempt."

"That's so sad."

"It's also unfair."

"I mean it's so sad about Joey. I hope he's going to be okay. Did she say what he did?"

"No." I realize now that I forgot to ask. I was so defensive that I totally forgot to be concerned about Joey. What is wrong with me?

"Well, I'm going to swing by your house and pick you up," she tells me. "We'll both be late, but that's the breaks. In the meantime, why don't you call Jess back and ask her how we can be praying for Joey."

I agree, but as soon as I hang up, I'm not so sure. I mean Jess sounded pretty mad at me. Why do I want to go poke that hornets' nest again? Still, I know that BJ will ask. So I dial Jess's cell-phone number and wait, hoping maybe she's turned it off.

"*What?*" she says sharply, which tells me she's using her caller ID.

"Hey, I'm sorry," I begin. "And I'm really sorry about Joey too. Is there anything I can do?"

"Not really."

"Well, I'd like to be praying for him, Jess. How's he doing? Is he going to be in the hospital for long?"

"He cut his wrists," she says in a flat-sounding voice. "He lost a lot of blood, but they have him on IVs and stuff. They're going to be keeping him in the psych ward to observe for a couple of days."

"Oh, because they're worried about him doing it again?"

"Pretty much."

"Well, I really am sorry, Jess. And I will be praying for him. And BJ will too. And if there's anything we can do—"

"Maybe you could start treating him like normal again," she says in a tired voice. "For you that might mean you should start teasing him again, not that I recommend it."

"What?"

"Look, Ramie, we're people too. Just like you. We need the same kinds of things that you do. We need to be loved and accepted and treated like normal human beings. Is that too hard to grasp?"

"No, of course not."

"Fine."

"Well, take care, Jess."

"Thanks."

I'm fighting back anger as I hang up. Why is she talking to me like that? I thought we'd made some progress, but now she's acting like I'm the enemy. Am I really that bad?

BJ's outside honking, so I grab my stuff and race out. As soon as I'm in the car I start venting about how Jess talked to me.

"She pretty much told me off." I pause to catch my breath.

"That's so weird. I mean after talking with her on Saturday, I felt kind of hopeful."

"Me too. But she sounded like someone else just now. Like I didn't even know her. All that talk about how people like *us* treat people like *them* . . . It was like she wanted to get into a big old fight right there on the phone."

BJ presses her lips tightly together, and I can tell she's thinking. "Was anyone with Jess? There at the hospital?"

"I think so. She mentioned that some kids from the gay alliance had gone to show support for Joey."

"I'll bet they were standing around listening to Jess while she was talking to you. She was probably trying to impress them."

"Maybe, but it was still pretty harsh."

"Jess is in a hard place. Think about it. One of her gay friends tries to kill himself, probably because he's been ostracized by family and friends after coming out of the closet. And there Jess is, trying to be supportive while other gay friends are looking on. She's probably acting tough for their sakes."

"I hope that's it. But even so, I hate to keep feeling like the lines are being drawn. Like this is the gay camp and this is the straight camp. And don't you dare step over that line."

When we get to practice, it seems that everyone has already heard about Joey's suicide attempt. And while some of the players' comments are compassionate, some are not. Following practice, I overhear several disturbing things in the locker room. And finally I get fed up.

"That's what happens when you let everyone know you're gay," a girl named Kelsey is saying to Amy. Kelsey's a senior who barely made varsity this year. In fact, I'm pretty sure the only reason she made it was because she's played every year and Coach Ackley felt sorry for her. "Better to keep your mouth shut," she continues. "I mean you go around and tell everyone and you're just asking for trouble."

"Yeah," agrees Amy. "Too bad someone can't just ship all the homosexuals off to some deserted island somewhere. Let them live their own lives and leave the rest of us normal folks alone."

Though I probably had that same attitude myself, and not so long ago, today I find it very offensive. Since I don't know Kelsey that well, I speak directly to Amy.

"You know, Amy," I begin, "It's hard to deal with this whole homosexual thing, but that comment you made about shipping them all off to some island is pretty harsh."

"Hey, it's just my opinion, Ramie. Don't get all PC on me."

"But what if your opinion hurts others? Like I know that people have said or thought the very same thing about me. You know, bigoted people who think that just because I'm biracial, I should go live somewhere else too."

Her eyes get wide now, but this seems to keep her quiet.

"Anyway, I just think it's a pretty unfeeling thing to say."

"Oh, I was only kidding, Ramie," she says quickly now. "You know me, the freaked-out homophobe."

"I know, but I'm thinking maybe we all need to lighten up on these guys. Like we should just get over it, you know?"

"Yeah," Amy nods. "I should probably learn to keep my big mouth shut."

"So, are you saying you think it's okay, Ramie?" says Kelsey. She stands up straight, looking me right in the eye. "I mean we've all been noticing how you and BJ have been hanging with Jess lately, acting like it's no big deal that she's a lesbian."

"Yeah. I guess we're hoping we can set a good example."

"Or maybe you guys are coming out too," she says in a slightly mocking tone. Then she laughs.

"I'm sure you think that's really funny, Kelsey," I tell her. "But I think it's pretty offensive."

"Why should *you* be offended?" she continues. "I mean on one hand you're saying that we need to accept homosexuals. But then on the other hand, you don't want to be associated with them. What's up with that?"

I consider this for a few seconds, wondering how I can get through to this girl. "So, do you accept *me?*" I finally ask her.

"Huh?"

"Do you accept me?" I repeat. The locker room gets pretty quiet now. Maybe the girls think we're about to start punching each other. Of course, I have no intention of getting physical. "I mean," I continue, "if you haven't noticed, my skin isn't exactly the same color as yours. So, I'm curious, do you accept me or not?"

All eyes are on Kelsey now. "Of course, I accept you, Ramie. What's your point?"

"So, are you biracial too?" Now I know this sounds ridiculous since Kelsey is a blue-eyed blonde, but I keep a very serious expression on my face.

"Nooo."

"Then isn't that kind of two-sided? I mean you say you *accept* me, but that doesn't mean you're *like* me." I watch her taking this in. "That sort of shoots down your theory about BJ and me, doesn't it?"

She shrugs.

"So maybe it's possible for us to accept Jess without being gay." I smile at her now. "Ya think?"

"Whatever." She turns away from me, acting like she's getting something out of her locker, but I know she just wants to get rid of me.

I look at BJ. She's grinning now, giving me a thumbs-up. "I think we should go visit Joey at the hospital today," I tell her in a voice that's loud enough for anyone who still wants to listen to hear.

"Sure," she says as she pulls on her jacket. "Sounds like a plan."

But first we head over to Starbucks to meet Nathan. Naturally, he's disappointed that Jess didn't make it, but we explain what's up and he seems really concerned.

"It's so sad that Joey would feel that desperate."

"Yeah, in a way it makes me worried about Jess too," I admit. "I mean I can tell that she's still depressed about how people are reacting to her. And I know things with her family are really stressed. It's gotta be so hard."

"I've really been giving this whole thing some very serious thought," he tells us, "and praying about it too. And I think it's high time that we, as Christians, start making an intentional move to restore relationships with people like Joey and Jess. I mean Jesus came for everyone. He didn't shun them because they were sinning. He just loved them and told them to follow him and to sin no more."

"Yeah," I say.

"I believe God is calling us to a ministry of restoration."

I nod. "I agree with you."

"Me too," says BJ. Then she tells him about my little confrontation with Kelsey in the locker room. "Ramie totally kept her cool too," she says finally. "I was impressed."

"That's awesome, Ramie. Good for you."

"I think it was God inspired," I admit. "But I suppose I do know what it feels like to experience prejudice. And, believe me, it feels horrible to be hated just because you're different. And it's disturbing that kids like Jess and Joey are really getting targeted because they came out."

"I don't know if it's just me," says BJ, "but it really seems to be a hot topic in the news lately too. It's like whenever I turn on the TV or read the paper, I'm hearing about people fighting about things like gay marriage or homosexuals who want minority rights. Did you guys see Bill O'Reilly last night?"

Neither of us had, so BJ gives us the lowdown. Much of the stuff about setting precedence and legislation and the Supreme Court goes over my head. But I think I basically get the drift.

"Even though I believe we need to reach out to homosexuals, it's still a confusing issue for me," I say. "I mean it's hard to balance being a Christian and having convictions against loving everyone no matter what. I mean we don't want to appear to be soft on sin, do we?"

"That's a good point, Ramie," says Nathan. "And I have to admit that even within our church leadership, not everyone agrees on how to deal with this issue. Believe me, it really is a hot button with some people."

"I wonder why that is."

"For starters, there's the whole fear thing. Some well-meaning people are convinced that homosexuals are dangerous—they almost classify them as criminals, thinking that they have some secret agenda to infect our whole society with their twisted ways of thinking."

"I've heard that some of them do have a political agenda," BJ points out. "I did a paper on it in sociology last year. There are gay groups that make a point of acting out just so they can get on the news. The idea is to be in the public's face until the public quits paying attention."

"I've heard of that too," says Nathan. "But I think it can backfire. Some of the stories, like the Boy Scout leader who turns out to be gay, only makes some people jump to the very worst conclusions. Some people just assume that the whole evil homosexual plan is to infect our children with sinful ideas. Or even worse, to sexually abuse them and infect them with things like HIV. And that's the kind of thinking that generates fear."

Of course, this Boy Scout comment only reminds me of Jess's experience at soccer camp. Not that Jess contracted some horrible disease, at least I hope not, but I'm sure it messed up her mind. "But things like that *do* happen," I point out. "I mean to some people. So maybe there is a reason to fear. Maybe we shouldn't let our guard down."

BJ looks at me, then nods. "Yeah. We actually heard a true story about someone who was sexually abused by a homosexual at a camp."

He frowns. "Unfortunately, I'm sure that those things do happen. But my point is that not every gay person is like that. They aren't all evil and twisted. Some of them are simply misguided and confused. And some of them really can't seem to help their own sexual orientation. They just want to live and let live, you know? Take Jess. Now she wouldn't try to hurt anyone, would she?"

"Well, she kind of hurt my feelings today," I admit.

"Yes. But you need to remember she's hurting too. Sometimes people hurt others when they're hurting."

"I know that's true, but I'm still worried about Jess. She seemed to be opening up to us on Saturday. And now this thing with Joey . . . well, it seems to have set her back."

"We thought we might go over to the hospital after this," BJ tells him. "Try to show some support for Joey, to let him know that we accept him, you know?"

"That's a great idea. Would you like me to come with you?"

So we agree to meet over there. But before we leave Starbucks, Nathan leads us in prayer.

"And remember," he says as we're going to our cars, "we are ministers of reconciliation. We are going to share Jesus' love and acceptance."

eighteen

I HAVE TO ADMIT THAT I'M FEELING PRETTY NERVOUS WHEN WE WALK INTO THE hospital. And when we enter the waiting area of the psychiatric unit, I am downright intimidated by the "diverse" crowd gathered there.

There are about twenty or more people loitering around the waiting area, and it's obvious that they are probably all homosexuals. Okay, I know that's pretty prejudicial on my part, but there's just something about them—the way they look or their clothes or the way they're talking—that sets off all kinds of alarms in me. And, sure, I don't like to judge appearances, but my first impression is that this could be a pretty rough crowd. Some of them might even be those militant in-your-face types that BJ was talking about earlier. I glance over at Nathan and BJ, and although I can tell they're not quite sure about this group either, Nathan puts on a confident smile and heads straight to Jess. BJ and I trail right behind him.

"Hey, Jess," he says. "I'm sorry to hear about your friend."

"We wanted to come by and see how he's doing," adds BJ.

"I told them a little about him," I say, almost feeling as if I need to apologize for this, or apologize for us coming. Should I have asked her first?

Jess's eyes narrow slightly as she carefully studies the three of us, as if trying to gauge why we are here. Then she glances back to her unusual assortment of friends, all of whom seem to be staring at us now.

"He's doing okay, considering," she says. "We're taking turns going in to see him. Only two visitors at a time and only for five minutes." She sighs. "But I don't think he'll want to see you guys."

"Are these your friends?" asks a very butch-looking girl that I've seen around school before. Her hair is about an inch long, spiked and tinted midnight blue, and she's wearing what looks like a motor-cycle jacket over a faded pink T-shirt that has Girl Power written across the front in felt pen. She has numerous silver studs piercing her eyebrows and what looks like a miniature black barbell hanging through the center of her lower lip. I'm sure her appearance is all about keeping people at arm's length from her, and it's working for me. I basically want to turn around and run in the other direction.

"This is Casey," says Jess.

Then Nathan introduces himself and us, sticking out his hand to shake, but Casey just ignores it, shoving both her hands into the pockets of her baggy jeans. "Are you guys friends of Joey?" she asks.

"We know Joey from school," I say. "I have some classes with—"

"Aren't you the one who teases him all the time?" she says to me.

"I used to tease him," I admit. "But I thought he kinda liked it. Sometimes he'd tease me back. I thought we were just being goofy."

"Goofy?" Her pierced brows draw together.

"You guys should go," Jess says in a quiet tone.

"Can't we say hi to Joey first?" BJ asks.

"Do you even *know* Joey?" Casey demands. "Or did you just come here to gawk?"

162

"I've known Joey since grade school," BJ tells her in a calm voice. "Ask him if you don't believe me."

"Well, I know he doesn't want to see any gay bashers," says Casey in an overly loud voice. Naturally this gets the attention of the other people in the room, and I can feel all their eyes on us now.

"We're not gay bashers," I tell Casey. "We're concerned about Joey and all the stuff that's been —"

"Sure," says Casey, "you're concerned now. Now that Joey has been so hurt by creeps like you that he couldn't take it anymore."

"You don't even know me," I tell Casey.

"I know who you are, Ramie," she snaps back at me. "Jess has told me more than enough about you."

I glance over at Jess now, wanting her to step in and defend me. But she just stands there with her arms folded across her chest.

"Jess and I are friends," I say in a weak-sounding voice.

Casey just laughs.

"Can someone please tell Joey that we'd like to see him," says BJ.

Now a guy steps up. He doesn't look like anyone from school, and I'm guessing he's in college. He's about my height, but very heavy. He has on an olive green army jacket, and the black knit cap pulled low on his brow only adds to the intimidation factor.

"Maybe you guys should just beat it," he says in a surprisingly calm voice. "It won't help anything for you to be here. You know?"

"I can understand that you guys might think we don't belong here," says Nathan. "But we really just wanted to reach out to you guys, to show you that we understand where you're coming from and that we accept and support you."

Jess looks surprised by this. "Seriously?" she says to Nathan. "Did the church send you as some kind of a peace-keeping mission?"

163

"We're here because we want to be here," he says. "And it is kind of a peace-keeping mission."

"Hey, there's Laura Myers from Channel Four news," says a guy wearing a trench coat.

Suddenly the attention is deflected from us and toward the small group of people just coming out of the elevator. Sure enough, there is Laura Myers, one of the news anchors, along with what appears to be a small camera crew.

They walk directly toward the waiting area and Laura inquires about Joey Pinckney. Then, satisfied that they're at the right place, she tells her camera guys to get ready, and they start setting up some lights and getting themselves into place for what looks like an impromptu news spot.

"Now anyone who wants to talk on camera will have to sign a release form afterward," she says as she drops a small pile of papers onto the coffee table. "Everyone just relax and act natural. This should only take a few minutes."

I glance at Jess. "Did someone call her?" I whisper.

She just shrugs. "I guess so."

Casey, who seems to be the self-appointed spokesman, is the first one to step up to Laura. "I'm ready to talk," she says. "My name is Casey Walters."

Laura nods and makes a note of this. "First I'll do a brief introduction and then we'll go directly to you. Just relax and tell the truth. Okay?"

Casey nods. "Okay."

"Here's a picture of Joey," says another guy, handing Laura a small photo. "He doesn't want to be interviewed about this yet."

"We're at St. Thomas General Hospital," Laura says to the camera now, "where sixteen-year-old Joey Pinckney of Greenville

High, the victim of a serious hate crime and gay bashing, is now recovering."

"Serious hate crime?" I say out loud. "Gay bashing?"

Laura Myers turns to me and frowns. "Is something wrong?"

"Well, this is news to us," I say, glancing at BJ and Nathan. "We never heard anything like that." I can feel Casey and the others glaring at me now. And I wonder if this was why they were so eager to see us go.

"Yeah," says BJ. "We heard that Joey tried to commit suicide."

"And who are you?" asks Laura.

"Just friends from school," I say meekly.

Casey laughs in a mean way. "They are definitely *not* friends of Joey or any of us, for that matter." She points to us. "These are some of the straight kids from school, the same ones that have given Joey a hard time for coming out." She points directly at me now. "Ramie even admitted as much just a few minutes ago."

"No," I say. "I didn't tease Joey about being—"

"Are you a gay basher?" Laura asks me. The camera is on me now.

"No," I say again. "I mean I had English with Joey and I used to tease him, but just in fun—"

"You teased Joey for being a homosexual?" Laura asks. "You humiliated him in front of classmates at school?"

"No! That's not what happened."

"Of course the gay bashers won't admit it on TV," says Casey, and the cameras turn to her now. "Gay bashers do their worst damage when no one is looking. It's a well-known fact that Joey has been constantly picked on since he came out. He told me numerous times that he didn't feel safe walking by himself down the halls at school."

"That's right," another kid shouts out. "Joey was always really freaked that he was going to be beat up by some psychotic homophobic moron."

"And this happened at school?" asks Laura. "The gay-bashing incident that led to Joey's life-threatening injuries?"

"Yes," says Casey. "It started at school."

"But it wasn't reported as a hate crime?" continues Laura, glancing at her notes. "The police show no record of a hate-crime report."

"No. Joey was too humiliated to tell the police what happened."

"Can you tell us what exactly happened?" Laura asks Casey. "This is a story that the public needs to hear."

"We don't know all the details," Casey begins. "But it started with a teasing incident at school. Joey was walking through the locker bays and somebody tripped him."

"Because he is gay?" asks Laura.

"Of course."

"And did that lead to a fight?" continues Laura. "Is that how Joey was beaten?"

"Yes," says Casey. "I think that's what he said."

"You think?" I echo, and Laura turns and gives me a warning look.

"Are you covering a story or creating one?" I say to Laura. "Because this sounds like a complete fabrication to me." I turn and look at Jess now. "You told me that Joey tried to kill himself."

Jess just glares at me.

"Besides," I continue. "School's been out for four days. When was Joey admitted to the hospital?"

"I think there may be a misunderstanding going on here," says Nathan, finally stepping up to Laura.

"Who are you?"

"I'm just a youth pastor, a friend to some of these kids—"

"You're not a friend to any of us!" yells Casey. "I'll bet you came here to see if you could preach at us. You probably want to save us from our sinful, aberrant, and immoral lifestyles, right?"

And then the waiting room just seems to erupt. Names are called and voices are raised and the whole time the cameras are going until finally some hospital security guards put an abrupt end to everything, telling us all to leave.

"Take it outside," one of the guards tells Laura Myers. "We have patients who came here to get well. Take this outside or we'll have you all arrested."

Nathan nudges BJ and me. "Come on," he tells us, and we follow him down a hallway to a different elevator. "We better get out of here," he says as he presses the button and waits.

"What happened?" BJ asks.

"They obviously want the media to think that Joey is the victim of a hate crime," says Nathan. "Although how they think they can get away with it is beyond me." He pulls out his cell phone as we get into the elevator. "But as soon as we're out of here, I plan to give Channel Four a quick call and hopefully a heads-up to whoever is over Laura Myers."

"Better not make the call while any of those nuts from upstairs are around to hear you," says BJ. "That Casey chick really scares me."

"It's so sad to think of Jess being connected with people like that," I say as the elevator shoots down to the lobby.

"You can't judge them all by just one girl's actions," Nathan warns us as we exit the elevator.

"But you saw them," I point out.

"I did," he says. "And I was really watching some of them pretty closely, trying to figure out how they were feeling and where they were coming from. And I was especially watching when the TV crew got there and things started getting crazy. Some of those kids, including Jess, were not a bit comfortable with what was being said. Some of them looked just as shocked as we were."

"Well, that's a comfort," I say as we hurry outside.

"You girls get out of here," he tells us. "I don't think any good will come out of a confrontation where tempers are flaring. But call me later, okay? I have some ideas."

"Do you think it will make the news?" I ask.

"I hope not." He waves as we hurry off to our cars.

"That was like so totally random," says BJ as she unlocks her VW. "Really, really freaky weird."

"I hope Nathan's right," I say as I get in. "I hope that they're not all involved in that lame hate-crime scheme."

"It looked like Casey and that dude in the army jacket were the ones behind it," she says as she pulls out of the parking lot. But as she drives past the hospital, we see the TV crew and the others now gathering out front. It appears they're going to continue their bogus news story without us.

"Man, I sure hope Nathan can talk some sense into Laura's boss. Can you imagine what a mess it will be if that hinky story makes it to the news?"

As it turns out, the story does make it to the local news. Only it's even worse than we imagined. The segment shows footage of the whole bunch of us, all yelling at each other and looking like we're about to get into a knock-down drag-out fight. The clips, taken out of context, really depict both BJ and me as serious bigots and hypocrites. Then there are clips where the gay-alliance kids describe being persecuted and threatened and beaten, which really makes it look like this town is full of those psychotic, homophobic morons that the kid in the army jacket was talking about. And it really paints the high school in a bad light.

I immediately get on the phone, trying to call Nathan, but I have to leave a message. Then I call BJ.

"Can you believe it?" I demand.

She lets out a groan. "What are we going to do, Ramie? We look like a couple of deranged homophobes."

"Can you imagine what someone like Amy or Kelsey will be saying to me tomorrow?" I say. Just then I hear the beep that tells me someone is trying to call. "I got another call," I tell her. "Maybe it's Nathan. He said he had an idea."

"Like his idea for calling Laura's boss?"

"Yeah, right." Then I tell her good-bye and take the next call, which turns out to be Mitch.

"Hey, I just saw you on the six o'clock news. What's up with that?"

"Can you believe it?" Then I try to explain what happened and how it got so out of hand and how Nathan was going to fix everything. "I feel like we're fighting a hopeless battle," I finally say. "And the reason we went in there today was just to make peace."

He laughs. "It's like I told you, babe, you should just stay out of the fray. Some of those homos can get pretty crazy. And it sounds like your old buddy Jess is just one of the crowd."

"It's just so hard to believe."

"Wake up and smell the coffee, Ramie."

"Maybe you're right."

"Of course I'm right."

"I'm just so tired of it. I wish everything would just go back to normal."

"What is normal?"

"You know, the way it was before. I wish that gay-alliance meeting had never happened."

"And that everyone would just go back into the closet and shut up?"

"Yeah." And, okay, so I guess I'm just as much of a hypocrite as Amy and Kelsey were today, maybe even more. I feel like a failure.

"I know how we can help you to forget about all this crud, Ramie," he says. "Why don't you let me take you out for some dinner and a movie—a movie that I promise won't have anything to do with homosexuality, okay?"

I gladly agree. I leave Mom a note and change my clothes and suddenly I'm looking forward to the great escape. Just an evening with Mitch and some good entertainment. Why not?

But later on, I'm cringing in my seat in the movie theater, wondering why on earth Mitch would bring me to see a piece of garbage like this—and what is it rated anyway? I realize that sexual immorality is all around me. It's like the entire culture is permeated with this crud. It's like I can't escape it. And, sitting there in the dark theater, I actually begin to cry. I feel like I'm not just crying for myself either, I am crying for everybody. How did we get to this low place? Why have we become a nation that's drowning in immorality? What has plunged us down this slippery slope? Is there any way out?

Deciding that the only thing I can do is on a personal level, I stand up and walk out of the theater. Okay, I'm sure that my decision to boycott a sleazy film after paying to see it isn't going to change the world, but it might change me. I stand out in the lobby, waiting to see if Mitch is going to come out and join me here. But then I suspect he thinks I'm using the ladies' room, so I go and sit down on a bench by the door and just wait. I mean wouldn't he get concerned after, say, twenty minutes have passed and I haven't returned? What if I was seriously ill? Or if I'd been kidnapped? Finally, in complete frustration, I call my mom.

"I'm sorry," I tell her. "But you've always told me that if I get into a situation where I feel uncomfortable, I'm supposed to call you."

"Of course," she says.

Then I briefly explain what's going on and she says she'll be here in a few minutes. In the meantime, I call Mitch's cell phone, which is turned off, and inform him of my whereabouts and not to bother calling since I won't be answering.

On my way home with Mom, I tell her about the hospital scene and Channel Four News. "It'll probably be on again at eleven."

She kind of laughs. "Actually, Rob from work already called and said he thought he'd seen you on TV."

"What else did he say?"

"That it wasn't good, and that he was shocked, and that I needed to have a talk with you."

"Go ahead," I tell her. "Take your best shot."

"No, I think you've explained it, Ramie. I just don't see how Channel Four thinks they can get away with something like that. Did you sign a release form?"

"No," I say suddenly. "Laura threw some papers on a table, but things got crazy and we had to leave. I never signed one. Neither did BJ."

"Then you guys might want to give Channel Four a call. Tell them that you're talking to your attorney about defamation of character." She laughs as she pulls into our driveway. "That might get their attention."

"Or, at least it might get them to retract what they said today." I glance at my watch to see that it's getting close to eleven now. "But not in time to miss the news tonight."

We hurry into the house, where I'm forced to watch the horror story all over again. And Mom even records it. "Just in case we need evidence," she tells me. "Or if you want to think about a career on TV. You actually look pretty good, Ramie. The color of your sweat-shirt really complements your skin tone."

"Thanks," I say in a flat tone. "I'm sure I'll want to watch this piece again and again."

The funny thing is that I do watch it again. But this time I pray first, and I ask God to help me to watch the whole report with an open mind. I do fast-forward through some of the overblown snip-pets and out-of-context comments. But I listen carefully as Laura Myers wraps up her piece by giving some alarming statistics.

"According to one survey, one out of two homosexual youths will endure verbal abuse, and 16 percent will suffer physical assault. But perhaps one of the most shocking discoveries of this study is that our public schools are the most dangerous place for homosexu-als. Seventy-four percent of the reported gay bashing occurred in elementary and middle schools, but that figure rises to an alarm-ing 89 percent in high schools. What happened to Joey Pinckney this week was wrong and tragic, but it's also a warning to everyone. Until school officials begin to enforce a zero-tolerance approach that protects all students from hate crimes and acts of discrimination, no one will be safe. This issue is no longer simply one of sexual moral-ity, it's about the schools' responsibility to ensure the health and safety of the students under their supervision."

As I turn off the TV, I think maybe she's right. Okay, maybe she didn't get all her facts straight, and I'm not too pleased with how she portrayed BJ and me, but in some ways she was able to say what I've been trying to say (to people like Coach Ackley and some of my teammates) and maybe somebody will actually listen to her.

nineteen

I'M ONLY MILDLY SURPRISED WHEN MITCH DOESN'T CALL ME THE NEXT DAY. I can't remember exactly what I said to him, but I'm sure I must've sounded angry. Maybe even a little neurotic. Whatever. Right now I have other things to obsess over.

Nathan called both BJ and me. First he apologized for not being able to get Laura Myers straightened out before the news hit the airwaves. But then I told him about how, despite being publicly humiliated like that, I thought Laura actually made some good points.

"I'm glad you could see that," he says. "That's why I want you and BJ to be on our panel."

"Panel?"

"Yes, I already spoke to Pastor Bryant about having an event at the church. It would be a way to bring the problem of homosexuality to the open forum. And he agreed. We've decided to have it on Saturday, December 29. Jeanie, the church secretary, is handling publicity. I've already called Laura Myers at Channel Four. I explained that we'll have a discussion panel and that we plan to openly discuss gay issues and concerns. We're calling it Christianity Meets Homosexuality." He kind of laughs. "That should get some attention. Anyway, it sounds like Channel Four will cover it, and I'm sure the church will be packed."

"Wow. That should be interesting."

"I've also asked Jess to participate, along with some of her gay-alliance pals."

"Did she agree?"

"She said she'd think about it."

"Maybe you could have Joey Pinckney on the panel too," I suggest.

"That's a fantastic idea, Ramie. Do you want to ask him?"

"I, uh, I don't know."

"But you're willing to participate?"

"Yeah, sure. I guess." Okay, I'm thinking this could be scary.

"And I like your idea about Joey. Pray about asking him. Hearing Joey's experience would be a great opportunity."

I want to ask, "Opportunity for what?" but BJ is outside honking for me. "I've got to go to practice," I tell Nathan. "Thanks for getting this thing together."

"I'm so glad I don't have to go to practice alone," I tell BJ as she drives toward the school.

"Yeah. Me too."

"After the way the news made us look last night, it'd be easy to just go hide under a rock."

"I told Nathan pretty much the same thing this morning when he called about the forum. He said we should think of this as our chance to be clowns for God."

I force a laugh. "Yeah, right. That sounds like a barrel of fun."

"But it did give me an idea," she says. "I thought maybe if we go in there today with some kind of a battle plan, maybe it would be easier."

"You have something in mind?"

"Well, you know what's going to happen. Everyone's going to

be pointing the finger at us, making fun of us, calling us hypocrites. You know, the basic juvenile MO."

"I know."

"How about if we make a pact right now that we will not say a single word back to them. Not one word to any of them in response to any of this. We'll just give them these blank looks but not a word."

I consider this. "It's an interesting idea, BJ. And it would be a good test of self-control for me, since I tend to shoot off my mouth pretty easily. But what do you think it will accomplish?"

"First of all, it'll give them a chance to get it all out there. Plus they'll probably end up saying some stupid stuff and maybe even feel bad for it later. But mostly, when we know we have their attention, like maybe after practice in the locker room, we can ask them if they want to know the real story—you know, what really happened."

"Aha."

"And then we'll tell them."

"But what if Jess is there? And what if she denies our story? And what if it turns into a big ugly brouhaha?"

BJ sighs. "If Jess does something like that . . . well, I think it means she's really changed. And maybe it means we can't trust her anymore. But hopefully that won't be the case."

I decide it's worth a try. "Besides," I tell BJ, "I think it'll be a relief to keep my mouth shut for a change."

"Yeah, maybe we can just focus on practice and improving our game."

"Wouldn't that be nice?" I tighten the Velcro on my wrist guard. I'm supposed to wear this thing for the whole season to ensure that I don't reinjure my wrist. But it really would be cool to just focus on playing basketball again—to forget about all this obnoxious stuff that just doesn't seem to want to go away.

I feel partly relieved and partly concerned when Jess doesn't show for practice today. And after silently enduring a bunch of stupid and snide comments about our news debut, pretty much as we predicted, the players seem to settle into a routine practice. Even the scrimmage seems to be pretty normal. But once we're back in the locker room, the comments about BJ and me on the news start flowing again. Still, we're keeping our mouths shut, just ignoring everyone as we get dressed.

"What's with you two?" Lauren finally asks. "Did you guys have a lobotomy or something?"

"Yeah," says Amy. "It's like return of the zombie girls. What's up?"

"You really want to know?" says BJ, and everyone gets pretty quiet.

"Yeah," yells Kara from the other side of the room. "What kind of game are you two playing anyway?"

"We'll only tell you if you'll listen," says BJ. And to my relief, she quickly summarizes what really happened at the hospital.

"Yeah," says Lauren, "I thought that was kind of weird that they were saying that Joey was the victim of a hate crime when we'd already heard it was a suicide attempt."

"What a setup," says Amy. "I can't believe you guys got yourselves into something so dumb."

"Would it have been better to have just ignored the whole thing?" I ask, remembering the advice that Mitch gave me. "Should we all be like ostriches and stick our heads in the ground?"

"Might be better than getting your head bit off," says Amy.

"Or being part of some gay-alliance scam," adds Kara. "I can't believe they want to cover up that Joey tried to kill himself, calling it a hate crime. What a bunch of jerks."

"If it was a hate crime, it's probably because Joey hated himself," says Kelsey. "Can't blame him there."

"See!" I point at her. "That's just it. That's why we have this kind of problem in the first place."

"Huh?" Kelsey glares at me as she pulls on her jeans. "What are you talking about?"

"Maybe they're right," I say. "Maybe Joey's suicide really is the result of a hate crime. I mean, isn't it possible that someone really did do something to him, something humiliating or embarrassing or hurtful? We see and hear stuff like that all the time at school. Didn't you hear those statistics on the news last night? Laura Myers said public school was the most dangerous place for homosexuals. Doesn't it make you guys feel bad?"

"If that's true," says Lauren, "if something did happen to Joey, something that made him want to kill himself, maybe it really would be considered a hate crime. I heard about a girl who got bullied so badly, at school and through e-mail, that she finally did kill herself. And she left a note saying why. And now her parents are pressing murder charges against the other girls."

"I wonder if Joey's parents could press charges?" says BJ as she ties her shoes.

"I guess that makes sense," says Amy. "I have heard that homosexuals have a really high suicide rate. You figure it's just because they're so miserable, but maybe it's because they get picked on so much."

Then BJ tells everyone about the forum we're going to have at our church after Christmas, inviting anyone who wants to learn more about this whole thing to come.

"It's just going to be people sharing their opinions and experiences in regard to homosexuality," she tells them. "Some gay, some straight. And hopefully we'll see how it all balances out with Christians and the Bible."

"Will there be a big fight at the end?" teases Amy.

"Hopefully not," I tell her. "But you never know."

This is our last practice before Christmas, and some of us start handing out cards, and then everyone is telling everyone to have a Merry Christmas, and then to our surprise the JV coach brings us out a big platter of cookies that Coach Ackley's wife made for us. I'm amazed at how the atmosphere in the locker room can instantly transform from animosity to good cheer, just like that. If only it could be like this always!

As BJ is driving me home, I tell her about my idea to invite Joey to be on the panel.

"That would be great," she says. "Are you going to ask him?"

"I don't know." I'm remembering what that Casey girl said about me teasing Joey, the way she made it seem like I picked on him because he was gay. But I just picked on him because he was Joey. I always thought he liked the attention.

"Why don't we do it together?" she suggests.

"Yeah, that might be okay."

"Why not do it now?"

"*Now?*" Visions of what happened yesterday flash through my head.

"Yeah. I'm not busy right now. And maybe it will give Joey something to look forward to, a chance for him to be heard."

"Do you think he's still in the hospital?"

"Why don't you call and find out?"

It turns out that he's still in the hospital. Even so, I'm not convinced paying him a visit is such a great idea. "What if all those guys from the gay alliance are there?" I ask BJ.

"Well, I doubt that the news will be there today. And don't you think that's why they were acting like that? I mean for the most part. Kind of a setup, you know?"

"Maybe." Still, I'm not so sure. News or no news, I don't want a run-in with that Casey chick again.

"Come on, Ramie," she urges me as she takes a turn toward town and the hospital. "I think the Lord wants us to do this. In fact, let's pray about it as I drive. Let's ask God to be in control and to bring some good out of this thing."

I can't help thinking we did that yesterday, but I don't say this. Instead, we both pray. We ask God to be in control. We ask him to use us to love others and to help us to control our tongues. We ask that we'll just be a good witness for him.

twenty

"LET'S SWING BY LE CHATEAU," I SAY TO BJ ON OUR WAY TO THE HOSPITAL. "It's the next street. Turn right."

"You hungry?"

"No. But maybe we should take something to the others. Remember how that cookie platter cheered everyone up in the locker room?"

"Great idea!"

"Must've been a God thing," I tell her as we go inside the sweet-smelling bakery and pick out what seems to be an array of tempting holiday treats. And it's amazing how carrying this pink box of confections gives me a little more confidence when we go into the hospital this time.

"There might not be anyone here," BJ says as she pushes the elevator button. "Then we can share some with Joey and take the rest home."

But when we get to the waiting area on Joey's floor, about a dozen or so of the same crowd are still hanging out. It almost feels as if they're here to guard him, as if they think he'll be in danger if they leave. Well, at least they're loyal.

"Merry Christmas," I say as we walk toward them. They watch us with narrowed eyes and tight lips.

"We brought treats," announces BJ.

"Yeah," I say, "No hard feelings about yesterday, okay?" I set the box on the coffee table and open it up. "They're from Le Chateau," I tell them.

"Probably poisoned," says Casey from where she's standing at a distance, arms folded across her chest as she leans against a post next to the couch.

"Nope," I tell her as I remove a cookie and take a bite.

"Why are you doing this?" Jess asks me as she eyes the box of cookies with suspicion.

"We want to be friends," I tell her. "We want to understand where you guys are coming from."

"Are you guys for real?" asks the heavy guy with the knit cap.

I smile at him. "Yep."

So he reaches for a cookie and takes a bite. "These are good," he says to his friends, and soon most of them are eating. Amazingly, almost like the scene in the locker room, the atmosphere in here begins to lighten up. Okay, we still take some jabs, and Casey and another girl refuse to come within ten feet of us. But BJ tells everyone about the forum and how we hope that Joey will be well enough to talk.

"We think people need to hear his story," I tell them. "They need to hear how he felt, how it feels to be treated like he was. And how it could drive a person to a place where he'd want to take his own life."

"Why?" snipes Casey from her position by the post. "So you guys can figure out a better way to attack Joey, a way that will make him succeed at killing himself next time?"

BJ and I just look at her.

"They didn't attack Joey," says Jess in a slightly exasperated tone.

"Maybe not physically," says Casey. "But you told me yourself that Ramie teased Joey a lot."

Jess rolls her eyes. "Yeah, Ramie is like that. She's been teasing Joey since middle school, back when he used to give her a bad time for not getting algebra. She teased him for being a brainiac. It's not about being gay, Casey."

Casey just glares at Jess, then she nudges the butch-looking girl beside her, and they both just walk off. A couple of the other girls follow. And now it's just Jess and us and the guys left.

"That's the problem with some of the gay chicks," says a guy on the couch. He's wearing a yellow shiny shirt and has his legs crossed in a slightly effeminate way. "They can be so aggressive."

The other guys laugh. But I glance at Jess and she's not laughing.

"Yeah, give me a straight girl to hang with any day," says another guy. "I mean a straight girl who gets me and who likes to shop for shoes." More laughter.

Now Jess walks off. I glance at BJ, then follow her.

"Jess?" I call.

She turns around and she looks close to tears. "What?"

"Is this our fault?"

She shrugs.

"I'm sorry," I tell her as the two of us stand in a quiet corner of the hallway. "Maybe we should just go."

"Maybe."

"We just wanted to see if we could patch things up. I mean after yesterday. We don't want this to be like a war. It's like we're trying to build a bridge, you know. We're trying to love you guys the way Jesus would. But maybe we're not helping."

"I don't know."

"We wanted to invite Joey to be in the forum."

She nods to the door across from us. "That's his room. And it looks like no one's in there now. Go ahead and ask him."

"Do you want to come in?"

She shakes her head. "No. I've already talked to him today."

"You sure it's okay if I just go in?"

"Yeah. They're pretty relaxed about him today. He's not on suicide watch or anything now." She gives me a little shove. "Go ahead, Ramie."

So I slowly walk into his room. But I'm thinking this is not how I planned to do this. BJ was supposed to come with me. But then I'm standing there, at the foot of his bed, and he's looking at me with a curious expression.

"What're you doing here, Ramie?"

"I came to see if I could bribe you to do my geometry homework, Joey. Whadya think?"

He actually laughs. "I think you could use a brain transplant, but since I survived and would have donated my brain to science anyway, you'd be out of luck."

"Well, you know what they say about brains, don't ya?"

"No, what?"

"Well, this guy needed a brain transplant and had two models to choose from. One belonged to a basketball player who never finished high school, and it was selling for a million bucks. But the other one had belonged to a math genius and was on sale for only $1.99." I pause so he can take this in. "So the guy who needed the brain transplant asked why the big price difference. And the salesman told him that the basketball player's brain was as good as new. It had hardly been used."

Joey laughs and asks if I want to sit down. So I do.

"You know, Joey, I'm sorry if I teased you and—"

"No way, Ramie, don't ever be sorry for that," he says quickly. "I love it when you tease me. Sometimes that's the only fun kind of attention I get."

"Really? You don't mind?"

"Not at all. I mean how many times have I called you a sports geek or a girl jock or whatever? You don't really get mad at me, do you?"

"Of course not. And that's kinda what I thought too, but then everyone else was acting like I was this terrible unfeeling person. Like it was my fault."

"No way, Ramie. Don't worry. It's not because of you."

"Look, Joey, I won't pretend that I understand the whole gay thing. I mean I seriously do not. But Jess used to be my best friend. And I care about her. And I care about you too. And I'm trying to find a way to wrap my head around this thing. You know that I'm a Christian, right?"

"Yeah."

"And it's like I feel torn. I mean on one hand, we're supposed to take a stand against sin. But on the other hand, we're supposed to love everyone. And it can be confusing."

Joey doesn't say anything.

"But more and more, I'm thinking about what Jesus did. And mostly I think that he loved people. He spent time with people. He hung with them wherever they were at. And that's what I'm trying to do. BJ is too. But it's still tricky, you know?"

"I know."

"Okay, I realize I'm just talking about myself now, Joey. And I know you're hurting. Is there anything I can do to help?"

He kind of smiles. "Just keep being yourself, Ramie."

"Well, there's room for improvement." Then I tell him about the forum our church is having after Christmas. "We'd really like you to be a part of it."

"I don't know."

"I can understand how it might be hard," I tell him. "But the purpose is to inform people about the problems. People need to understand how the teasing hurts. We need to find ways to bridge this gap. Especially between Christians and homosexuals. Do you see what I mean?"

"I guess so."

"Well, there's no hurry. Just think about it, okay?"

"Yeah, sure." Then he looks toward the door and I can hear someone coming in.

"Hey, it's one of the straight chicks," says a guy's voice behind me.

I turn around and smile at the guy in the shiny shirt. "My name is Ramie," I tell him.

"And I'm Jeremy and this is Aaron." And we all shake hands.

"Ramie and that other straight chick brought cookies," says Jeremy as he hands Joey a couple that are wrapped in a napkin. "Thought we'd sneak some in for you."

"Thanks." Joey smiles. "Beats this hospital food."

"Well, I better go," I say. "I heard there's a limit on visitors."

"Thanks for coming," says Joey. And I think he really means it.

"Merry Christmas," I call out as I head for the door.

"She's pretty," says Jeremy when he thinks I'm out of earshot.

"Did you see her shoes?" says Aaron.

I laugh as I go down the hall. I think it might be easier for me to get along with gay guys than lesbians.

"How'd it go?" asks Jess from behind me.

I jump to hear her voice, then stop and turn around. "You scared me."

"Sorry. How's Joey?"

"He's cool."

She nods. "Yeah. He is."

"And you were right."

"About?"

"The teasing thing. Joey agreed that it was totally mutual. And he made me promise not to quit. So I won't."

"Yeah. Sorry about the way that went yesterday. It was so blown out of proportion. And I know that I was part of the problem."

"It was kind of shocking."

"Well, I'm sure you know by now that it was all planned."

"We had our suspicions."

"We met and kind of got a strategy. It was Casey's idea."

"Oh."

Now we're coming back to the waiting area, and Casey and the other girls have returned and are sitting around talking and stuff. But BJ isn't around.

"Where's BJ?" I ask.

Casey shrugs. "Why should we care?"

"She just asked you a simple question," says Jess. "You could at least give her a civilized answer."

"Are you saying I'm uncivilized?" demands Casey, standing up and looking Jess right in the face.

"Hey, if the shoe fits."

Casey takes a step toward Jess, and I honestly think I can see fire in that girl's eyes.

"Never mind," I say quickly, grabbing Jess by the arm. "We'll find her." I tug Jess along with me.

"You're getting awful cozy with the straight chicks," calls Casey. "You converting them or are they converting you?"

"Shut up!" Jess calls back at her.

Their laughter floats behind us as we make our way to the elevators. Then, as we're waiting there, a girl comes around from the other side. She's one of their group, but one of the quiet ones. I don't know her name.

"BJ said she would be in the coffee shop," she whispers to me as the doors to the elevator open.

We thank her, then get in and go down.

"Who's that?" I ask.

"Morgan."

"She seems nice."

Jess shrugs.

"I mean for a friend," I say quickly, wondering if I've been misunderstood. "I didn't mean you should ask her out."

Jess laughs now. "Don't worry. She's not my type."

"What is your type?" I ask as the doors open.

"I'm not sure yet."

"Oh." Now for some reason that makes me feel relieved. And I guess I'm hoping that Jess is not involved with anyone yet. I'm hoping that she'll get some help first. But I have no idea how to say something like this, or if I even should. We find BJ at the coffee shop, and we all sit down together and talk.

"I'm so confused," Jess admits. "I mean life almost seemed to be making some sense after I talked to you guys on the bus, after I told you, well, you know . . . But then this whole thing with Joey happened and it felt like being blindsided. And everyone was so angry and I just kind of got swept along."

"I can understand that," says BJ.

"You need counseling," I remind her.

"Nathan really wants to talk to you," says BJ. "And we can still go with you too, if that helps."

"Maybe."

"Jess," I begin. "You can get mad at me about this if you want to, but I talked to my mom about what happened to you."

She just shrugs. "I figured you would."

"But you know my mom," I say quickly. "And if anyone is cool about homosexuality, she totally is. And, of course, she immediately offered to talk to you or your family if it would help, but she said you definitely do need counseling. She said not to put it off either. She was very clear about it. She said what happened to you at soccer camp was totally wrong and that it's had a huge impact on your life. You can't ignore it, Jess."

"I know."

"And we're here for you," says BJ. "We're still your friends, Jess. You know that, don't you?"

"I guess."

BJ looks at her watch now. "Well, I should go. I promised my mom that I'd help her to get things ready for all the family that will be storming our house for Christmas Eve tomorrow night."

Then we actually hug Jess. And, okay, it feels a little weird. But I tell myself to get over it, and Jess really seems to appreciate it.

"Ramie?" she says just as we're leaving. "I know you probably won't want to now . . . I mean since things have changed . . . but you used to always come to our house on Christmas Eve, you know, while your mom goes to one of her crazy New Age winter parties . . . and I—"

"I'd love to come!" I say. "Really, I would. It would be so much better than one of those parties."

She smiles. "Cool."

"Yeah." I nod. "Totally."

And seriously, despite the tension that I know will be in the air at Jess's house, I really do love her family. I really would like to be with them.

twenty-one

"You're doing what?" Mitch asks me the next day when he unexpectedly stops by my house.

"I'm going to Jess's house for Christmas Eve," I tell him for the second time.

"Why?"

"Because she's my friend."

"Are you turning into a lesbian too?" he asks. Then he laughs like that's really funny. "Although I have to admit that I might get into that. I mean if you were one of those girls who swung both ways. It is kind of a turn-on for guys, you know."

"Mitch!" I stare at him with a shocked expression, thankful that we're sitting across from each other at the island in the kitchen.

"Oh, don't act so surprised."

"Then don't be so gross."

"Sorry." He makes his little-boy face, his hint that he wants me to forgive him. And while I can forgive him, I'm just not sure that I want to keep dating him.

"Sometimes I think we're not right for each other," I begin.

He frowns. "Oh, come on, Ramie. Just because I made a stupid joke. You know I didn't mean it."

"Maybe."

"I brought your Christmas present."

Okay, now this is making me nervous. Not only have I totally not gotten him anything (partly because I was mad and partly because I get the feeling this relationship is doomed), but I know I will really feel trapped if I accept a gift from him. And yet breaking up on Christmas Eve . . . isn't that a little harsh?

He's taking something out of his jacket pocket now. And judging by the box, it's jewelry. How can this be? He grins as he slides the long, narrow blue-velvet box toward me. "Sorry I didn't wrap it."

"I can't accept this," I tell him.

He frowns. "You haven't even opened it, Ramie."

I know. I push the box back toward him. "But I can't accept it."

"What do you—"

"I'm sorry, Mitch," I tell him in my firmest voice. "Everything has been so crazy lately. And I haven't even seen you since the other night when I ditched you at the movie."

"Well, you're right, that movie was pretty slimy. Sorry about that."

"I forgive you," I tell him. "But it's not just the movie, Mitch. It's you and me. We're so different."

"Vive la différence," he says hopefully.

"Yeah," I say. "Different can be good. But I am trying to be a strong Christian, Mitch. And when we started going out, I just assumed you were too."

"I never told you that."

I nod. "Yeah, you're right. You never did. I guess I just hoped it was true. Maybe I imagined it was true."

"But you knew where I stood, Ramie. I've always been honest about my faith—or my lack of it."

"I know. Maybe it was just the thing with Jess that kept me

going. Maybe it made me more desperate for a boyfriend than I should've been."

"So I've just been your wrist candy?" he says in a mocking way. "Your boy toy that you can use and then lose?"

"Oh, Mitch," I say. "You know that's not true. I really do like you."

He lets out a deep sigh, then looks at me with surprisingly sincere eyes. "I really like you too, Ramie. Seriously, you're the coolest girl I've ever been with. You're fun to talk to and great to kiss. I really thought we had something."

"I kind of thought we did too, Mitch. But now I think I was imagining most of it. Maybe you were too."

"So this is it? You're really breaking up with me?"

I nod. But even as I nod I am questioning this myself. Why? Why *am* I breaking up with Mitch?

He takes the velvet box and slips it back into his pocket again. "Well, guess I better go then."

I can hear the hurt in his voice, and it cuts through me too. "I'm sorry, Mitch," I tell him. "If things were different . . . I mean if we were more alike . . . if you believed what I believe . . ."

"Oh, forget it, Ramie." He just turns and walks away now. He goes straight for the front door and, without another word and without even looking back and no last kiss, he walks out of my life, slamming the door behind him.

I feel terrible. I feel just as bad as if he'd been the one who broke up with me. That's how much it hurts. I thought I'd be relieved to be done with this, but instead, as I peek out the front window and watch his Mustang driving away, I feel this utter sense of despair. What have I done?

I turn away from the window and go up to my room, slowly taking each step as I ask myself again and again, *What have I done?*

What have I done? I throw myself across my bed and fight off the urge to pick up the phone and call him. I want to tell him that I've made a huge mistake, that I'm sorry, and would he please come back? Would he take me back? I'm even asking myself what was in that blue-velvet box. Probably something I would've loved. How could I be so stupid?

And then I consider how this will make me look. What about my image? What will people think? I break up with Mitch on Christmas Eve and then go to Jess's house to celebrate. How does that look? And how can I be Jess's friend without having a boyfriend to hang onto? Won't people assume I'm a lesbian now? How can I do this without Mitch? That old desperate feeling reaches out and grabs me by the throat. How can I do this without Mitch? How can I do this alone?

I take in a deep breath and I remind myself that I am not alone. *I have God.*

So I get down on my knees and I tell God that I need him—I really, really need him. I tell him that I feel like I'm walking a tightrope and that one step to the right or the left and I will fall. And that's when I get this very vivid image in my mind. I see God holding my hand and promising me that as long as I hang on to him, I will not fall. And for the first time in a long time, I feel myself beginning to relax. I thank him and praise him for this image. I thank him that he's the only one who can walk me through this, the only one who can keep me from falling. And then I get this image of me falling, like I forgot and let go, but then I see his giant hand below me, catching me. And although I don't ever plan to let go of his hand, and I'll do everything I can to hang on, it is a comfort to know I have a safety net.

I don't tell my mom about breaking up with Mitch. I know she's in a hurry tonight. Her last counseling session ran long, and even though I'm helping her to fix her seven-layer dip for the party at Brenda's, she still needs to change her clothes. "You sure you don't want to come with me?" she asks.

"I already told Jess I'd come to their house," I tell her.

"That's so nice, Ramie. I'm so glad you and Jess have worked this thing out." Then she kisses me on the forehead. "You're such a good girl, Ramie. How did I get so lucky?"

I laugh. "I'm sure luck had nothing to do with it."

I don't tell anyone at Jess's house about my breakup either. It's not that I want to keep this thing top secret, it's just that it seems unnecessary to mention it just yet. And since no one asks, why should I bring it up? But as I visit with Jess's family, hoping my presence will reassure them that things are getting better, I feel this fresh new sense of freedom. It's like a weight has been lifted from me. And, okay, I'm still trying to navigate my way through the whole gay scene, but somehow I think it will be easier now. As if I'm less encumbered.

"I've called the people at the exit ministry," Mrs. LeCroix tells me in the kitchen. I'm helping her to refill a platter of appetizers.

"Oh." I glance over my shoulder to make sure Jess is not listening, since I just don't think she needs to hear this tonight. She seems to be pretty edgy anyway. She's already cried over an insensitive comment her sister made. Although I'm pretty sure I'm the only one who knows it. At least her brother, the one in seminary, seems to be acting fairly compassionate.

"The nice man at the exit ministry told me that while he understands my pain, Jessica will have to call the ministry herself before we can send her in for help." Mrs. LeCroix calmly tells me this as she arranges her meatballs in a neat row. "He said that it's no use coming unless the person wants help. Like you can lead a horse to water but you can't make him drink sort of thing."

I nod absently as I curl the pieces of ham like she told me to, slipping a toothpick in to keep them together. I only half listen as she continues going on and on about this place, how great it is, how badly she wants for Jess to go there. But I'm getting impatient now. It almost seems like the only thing Jess's mom cares about is getting things back to "normal." Like Jess isn't even a real person with real feelings. And, okay, I suppose I've been guilty of the same thing. But even so!

"Anyway," she continues, "I was thinking that maybe you could talk to her, Ramie. I really think Jessica would listen to you. You're a strong Christian girl and I think maybe you can convince Jessica that this perverted lifestyle is sinful and immoral and that she needs to get some—"

"You know, Mrs. LeCroix," I interrupt her so abruptly that she actually drops a meatball on the floor with a splat. "The thing is," I continue, "I'm just trying to love Jess. Trying to be her friend, you know. And I'm trying to love her unconditionally, the way God loves all of us, no matter what. I figure it's up to God to show Jessica what's best for her life." I pause and look at her. "Does that make any sense to you?"

And then I hear the sound of hands clapping behind me. I turn around to see Jess and her brother, standing in the doorway and watching us and clapping.

"Makes sense to me," Alex tells me as he comes into the kitchen and snatches a meatball off his mom's neat row, causing it to go crooked.

"Me too," says Jess as she takes another meatball.

Mrs. LeCroix looks slightly flustered, but at least she smiles as she straightens her meatballs. "I'm just trying to help, Jessica. You know I love you, don't you?"

"Yeah, Mom." Jess pats her mom on the back. "I know you love me, it's just that it doesn't always feel like it."

Things seem to lighten up in the LeCroix household after that. And as we sing Christmas carols and play silly games, it almost seems like Jess is having fun too, almost like she's her jolly old self again. And yet there are moments when I think I can see this shadow hanging over her. And I'm reminded that things have changed. She has changed. Maybe we've all changed.

"Thanks for coming tonight," Jess tells me as she drives me home. "I think it really helped having you there."

"Hey, I was glad to come," I say. "It was fun. Just like old times."

"And thanks for what you told my mom in the kitchen."

"No problem."

"Did you really mean it?"

"Of course."

"Thanks."

She's pulling into my driveway now. "Thanks for bringing me home," I tell her. "And for everything. And Merry Christmas!"

"I didn't get you anything for Christmas this year," she says.

"Oh, that's okay. I didn't either."

"But I have something . . ."

Okay, this makes me nervous. But I just take a deep breath and say, "What?"

"A promise that I'm going to get counseling. And I've decided I should start with Christian counseling, just like you suggested."

I smile. "Oh, that's a great Christmas present, Jess. Thanks!"

"But I was thinking maybe your mom could do some counseling with my parents. To help them to see outside of the box, you know?"

"Sure," I tell her. "My mom would be glad to help. You know that."

"And that won't bug you? I mean I know how you feel about your mom sometimes."

I consider this. "Okay, to be perfectly honest, it would've bugged me before. But I actually think my mom is right about some things. Not everything, of course." Then I laugh. "But knowing your parents and their convictions, well, I'm not too worried that she'll steer them wrong."

"Yeah, I can't exactly see them worshiping trees or taking up yoga or any other New Age kind of thing after talking to her." She smiles.

"Me neither." I open the door of her car now.

"Merry Christmas, Ramie."

"Merry Christmas," I call back as I get out of the car.

twenty-two

I'D LIKE TO SAY THAT THE FORUM AT OUR CHURCH RESOLVED EVERYTHING BEAU-
tifully. That Nathan's vision for Christianity Meets Homosexuality
was an enlightening and gracious gathering of diverse people from
all over the community, and that lives were changed, and that we
ended the meeting with an altar call followed by the holding of
hands as together we sang "Kumbaya." I wish I could say that the
whole thing was a total screaming success. Unfortunately, only the
screaming part of that statement would be correct.

Our well-intentioned meeting was more like *The Good, the
Bad, and the Ugly*. And although I'd like to say that the Christians
were "the good," that would not be entirely true. Oh, sure, some
of the Christians were very *good*, including Nathan, who tried
extremely hard to bring a peaceful understanding of gospel love
to the confused people of Greenville. But some of the Christians,
in particular those who misunderstood the publicity and erro-
neously believed that this was supposed to be an open forum
for Christians to rant and rail against the likes of Sodom and
Gomorrah, were in my opinion very, very *bad*. And, to be fair,
some of the gay-rights activists got downright *ugly*. Plus, the way
some of them were dressed, you'd think we were hosting a gay
parade or preparing for Mardi Gras.

Consequently, what was supposed to be a civilized and informative meeting quickly turned into a shouting match—a shouting match where no one was completely heard. Even as I watched the whole miserable thing on the eleven o'clock news later that night, it made absolutely no sense. There were snippets of an angry Christian man literally shaking his Bible as he yelled, "Keep your queers out of my kids' schools!" followed by two vividly gay men, embracing one another as they demanded their civil rights for a legal marriage.

Between accusations of physical gay bashing and actual verbal gay bashing, the whole thing turned into a pretty big mess. But if nothing else, I think our botched-up forum did provide something of a wake-up call for a lot of people in the community. Okay, maybe it was more like one of those obnoxious alarm clocks that you want to smash against the wall because it won't stop buzzing. But I was pleased that Jess's parents attended that meeting. And I could see that they were taken aback by some of the hostility shown to them by "fellow" Christians when they attempted to show their support of their daughter. Yes, they stood up for Jess. A small gesture, perhaps, but I could tell that Jess was deeply moved. Of course, her parents are still torn about this whole thing, and I'm sure they were pretty shocked by some of the skanky behaviors from a few of the openly gay community—specifically the ones who took advantage of all the in-your-face attention that the media gave to them when things got crazy.

Still, one of the best moments, albeit brief, was when some members of the youth group tried to express their desire to show Christ's love to gay teens in our community. Of course, this totally annoyed those who had hoped that the purpose of this meeting was to condemn all homosexuals and their evil influence, and perhaps to ban them from our schools and our town and maybe even our country forever.

"God judged Sodom and Gomorrah!" one irate woman yelled out toward the end. "And his judgment on the homosexuals of this age is AIDS. I predict that the Lord will wipe them out, every single one of them, until not one is left standing!"

When it was clear to see that this meeting was going nowhere but downhill, and fast, the church elders and pastors announced that it was time to quit. Cameras were shut down, members of the panel were ushered toward the back, and spectators dismissed. (Although some of the more determined rabble-rousers took their protests and accusations out to the church parking lot, where cameras were turned back on and some of the juiciest pieces of smut were taped to run on the late news.)

Meanwhile a bunch of us from the panel were still hanging out behind the scenes in the back of the sanctuary. Some members of the youth group were there, as well as some of the less rowdy members of the gay alliance, including Jess and Joey. And maybe the coolest part of this whole crazy evening was the way we just stood around and talked about everything that had just happened. I think we were all pretty stunned by some of the behaviors we'd just witnessed, most of it from the adults. And as we stood around, rehashing the whole strange event, we began to experience an ironic sense of unity.

"Let's do this again," BJ said, and others agreed.

"Maybe we can plan a meeting just for teens," I suggested.

"Yeah, we'll make sure not to tell the so-called grown-ups about it," said Joey. "Man, some of those people are really messed up."

Unfortunately, a few people from our church think that Nathan is the one who is messed up. Some of them are downright angry at our youth pastor, actually accusing him of brainwashing the youth group with his "pro-homosexual propaganda." And some are even calling for his resignation. Fortunately, Pastor Bryant is standing behind Nathan. At our Sunday service the following day, he even announced that he plans to continue this discussion of Christianity Meets Homosexuality, but within the confines of the congregation this time. "Apparently we still have a lot to learn before we go public," he apologized to the congregation.

I found out later, through Nathan, that part of the reason for Pastor Bryant's support of Nathan is due to his own son.

"How's that?" I asked.

"Apparently Mitch spoke out in my defense," Nathan told me.

"Why?" I wondered aloud, and then felt bad for doing so. Like why shouldn't Mitch defend Nathan? I certainly would.

Nathan just smiled. "Well, it may come as a surprise to you, but Mitch has suddenly gotten very spiritually hungry. He and I are going to start meeting for breakfast once a week."

"Cool."

Nathan smiles. "I think God has used your breakup with Mitch as a real attention-getter, Ramie."

I hope that's true. I know that I'll keep praying for Mitch. I do care about him, and I'd like him to start taking God and his own life more seriously.

***

We're back in school now, and while there are still those people who seem to thrive in making crude remarks and mean judgments, I've noticed that some of them are changing too. Even Kelsey has been a little kinder to Jess during basketball practice. And it seems some of the snide locker-room comments have died down a bit as well. Does this mean we've arrived? That we've figured this whole thing out and that everyone is happy now? Get real.

I think it just means that we're trying. And although some of my ideas about homosexuality have changed, I still believe that God didn't design us for same-sex relationships. I think he made us male and female for a reason, and not just for sex and reproduction either. I think God knew that men need women and women need men, and the world would be a mess if we all decided to become homosexuals. Not to mention there would be no one left on the globe after a few generations. But I also think that, like with many things, we get messed up, or our thinking gets confused, or maybe we've been sexually abused, or maybe we just want to rebel and go a different way. But that doesn't mean we can't change. That doesn't mean that God can't rescue us—*from anything*. And so I still believe that Jess could be rescued from living the rest of her life as a lesbian.

But I don't feel pressed to preach this at Jess every chance I get. I don't beat her over the head with scriptures and tell her to repent or go to hell. But I do encourage her to follow God, to spend time with him, and to continue her counseling, which she actually seems to like. Because I realize that most of all, God simply wants me to love Jess—*unconditionally*. He wants me to stand by her, even if I'm standing all by myself. And he wants me to know that, in the end, it's up to him to do the changing anyway. I can live with that.

reader's guide

1. Consider how these characters responded to Jess's revelation: Ramie, Mrs. Grant, Mrs. LeCroix, Jess's teammates. How would you react if your best friend told you he or she was gay? Why?

2. Why was it hard for Ramie to be a friend to Jess? Do you think Ramie was more selfish or more righteous? Explain.

3. What could Ramie have done differently to avoid hurting Jess while she sorted out how she felt about Jess's announcement? What did she do right?

4. What about Ramie's attitude toward Jess changed? Why? What stayed the same?

5. Ramie says, "More and more, I'm thinking about what Jesus did. And mostly I think that he loved people. He spent time with people. He hung with them wherever they were at. And that's what I'm trying to do. . . . But it's still tricky, you know?" Do you agree or disagree with Ramie's thinking here? Why? If you try to live the way Ramie describes, what's the trickiest part for you?

6. Do you think sexual orientation is a choice or just the way some people are? How does your answer affect the way you relate to gay people?

7. How do you think Jesus would relate to a homosexual? Would it be the same way that you relate? Explain.

8. If you, like Ramie, believe homosexuality is wrong or a sin, do you believe that it's any worse than other sins? Why or why not?

9. How did you feel when Ramie broke up with Mitch? Why?

10. Ramie used a tightrope to describe how she felt about dealing with homosexuality. Do you think this metaphor works? Explain.

TrueColors Book 11

Moon White

Coming in June 2007

One

"I AM NOT EVIL," I SAY QUIETLY, TRYING TO KEEP MY VOICE CALM FOR THE SAKE of those listening into what probably should be a private conversation. We're sitting in the cafeteria with about five hundred other kids at the moment, and I do not get why my best friend wants to pursue this topic right now.

"How can you say that, Heather?" she persists. "You're a witch!"

I try not to glare at her. "Come on, Lucy," I say in a light voice. "Don't show off your ignorance to everyone."

"You're calling *me* ignorant? You're the one who decided to become a witch."

"Lighten up," I tell her. "And quit calling me a witch, okay?"

"Fine," she snaps. "What would you call yourself then?"

I smile at Chelsea Klein. She's sitting next to Lucy and actually seems fairly interested in the strange twist our conversation just took. "All I'm doing is reading a book about Wicca," I say to Lucy. "No big deal, okay? That does not make me a witch."

Chelsea nods. "Yeah, lighten up, Lucy."

Lucy turns and glares at Chelsea now. "So are you saying that you think it's okay if Heather becomes a witch?"

Chelsea just laughs.

"I'm serious," says Lucy. "I mean you're a Christian too, Chelsea. At least I thought you were. Anyway, you used to go to youth group." Lucy frowns now, as if she's not sure what she's stepped into.

"What's your point?" asks Chelsea.

"My point is, do you think it's okay for Heather to be dabbling in witchcraft?"

"Dabbling in witchcraft?" I repeat. "Lucy, why are you making this into something that it's not?"

"Because I'm seriously worried about you, Heather." She shakes her head like she thinks I'm totally hopeless. "I mean you spend a couple of weeks in the British Isles and then come back with all these strange ideas."

"What strange ideas?" I ask.

"Well, for starters there's this whole vegan thing." Lucy rolls her eyes at my lunch tray. "I mean just a couple of months ago, your favorite food was pepperoni pizza, and now you won't even touch a milkshake."

"So you want to tell me what I should and shouldn't eat now?"

"That's not what I mean." Her forehead wrinkles and she looks more frustrated. "I'm cool with it, although I really don't get what your problem with dairy products is. I mean we're talking about milk, right?"

"I tried to explain to you about how I'm concerned with the inhumane treatment of dairy cows, but you wouldn't—"

"Whatever!" Lucy holds up her hands.

"You should be a little more tolerant, Lucy," says Chelsea.

"Yeah," agrees Kimball from next to me. "I happen to be a vegetarian myself. And I've been thinking about becoming a vegan. You have a problem with that, Lucy?"

"Maybe you want to make yourself captain of the food police?" teases Chelsea. "The CFP?"

"I wasn't even talking about food to start with," Lucy protests. "I mean, seriously, I don't care what you guys eat. That was just Heather's smokescreen. I *was* talking about Wicca and witchcraft and the fact that Heather wants to become a witch."

"And I told you that's not what's going on," I say, still trying to maintain some composure. I turn to Chelsea. "I just don't get why Lucy is acting like this. Why can't she just chill? Just because I'm learning about Wicca does not make me a witch."

"Look," Lucy says in an irritated voice. "If it walks like a duck and quacks like a duck, how can you prove it's not a duck?"

That actually makes me laugh. "Fine, Lucy," I tell her. "I can walk like a duck and quack like a duck, but that does not make me a duck. Okay?"

Lucy looks stumped and Chelsea and Kimball both applaud. "Well said," says Kimball.

"Thank you," I say, imitating Elvis, "thank you very much." But even as I say this, I feel badly for Lucy. I mean she is my best friend. Or rather she used to be. At the moment, I'm wondering if it's possible to outgrow some friends. Maybe the time comes when you have to cut your losses and move on. Still, I like Lucy. I don't really want to lose her. Maybe I need to just help her to understand that Wicca is no big deal. But I hadn't really planned on having a conversation like this in public.

"Look," I say to her in my patient voice. "I think the problem is that you don't really understand what Wicca is—"

"I know that it's witchcraft, Heather. And Pastor Hamilton taught a class about the occult last year, and Wicca was part of that, and I know that people into Wicca worship Satan and practice magic—"

"That's not true," I protest. "Wiccans don't even believe in Satan. How could we worship something we don't believe in?"

"So you admit that you're a Wiccan then?" says Lucy with a triumphant look in her eye, like she's caught me in the act.

"Maybe I am," I tell her.

She looks at Chelsea, then Kimball. "See, I told you she's a witch."

I just sigh.

"Well, she's a nice witch," says Chelsea sympathetically.

"Hey, can you put a spell on Marcus Abrams for me?" teases Kimball. "Or maybe just whip me up some kind of love potion?"

"Yeah, right." I just shake my head, wondering why I even try. "You guys just really don't get it."

"Well, explain it to us," says Chelsea.

"I would," I tell her, glancing at Lucy. "If I could manage to get out two sentences without being interrupted."

"Fine," says Lucy. "Explain away. I'll keep my mouth shut."

I study her for a moment, trying to figure out why she seems so angry. "Well," I begin slowly, "for one thing Wicca has a lot to do with nature and the seasons and the sun and the moon. It actually makes a lot of sense, when you think about it. And it's about doing good, not bad, and it's very ancient. It's been around for about thirty thousand years—"

"How can anyone know that?" challenges Lucy. "There's no recorded history that far back."

"I don't know," I admit. "But I've read that there are archaeological findings related to Wicca that go back that far."

"I don't believe it," she snaps.

"Obviously," I say.

"You said you were going to keep your mouth shut," Kimball reminds Lucy.

Lucy stands up now, slinging a strap of her bag over her shoulder. "Well, sometimes we need to speak out. And as a Christian, I can't just sit here and listen to my best friend talking about some Satanic religion and how it's so great." She looks down at me, then sighs. "I just don't know how you got so off track, Heather. But I still love you and I'll be praying for you." Then she turns away and walks off. And, okay, I realize that it's just Lucy's immaturity speaking, combined with her inability to accept change, and I shouldn't even react to her, but I feel like I've just been slapped.

about the author

MELODY CARLSON HAS WRITTEN DOZENS OF BOOKS FOR ALL AGE GROUPS, but she particularly enjoys writing for teens. Perhaps this is because her own teen years remain so vivid in her memory. After claiming to be an atheist at the ripe old age of twelve, she later surrendered her heart to Jesus and has been following him ever since. Her hope and prayer for all her readers is that each one would be touched by God in a special way through her stories. For more information, please visit Melody's website at www.melodycarlson.com.

Chloe

Diaries Are a Girl's Best Friend

MY NAME IS CHLOE, Chloe book one

Chloe Miller, Josh's younger sister, is a free spirit with dramatic clothes and hair. She struggles with her identity, classmates, parents, boys, and whether or not God is for real. But this unconventional high school freshman definitely doesn't hold back when she meets Him in a big, personal way. Chloe expresses God's love and grace through the girl band, Redemption, that she forms, and continues to show the world she's not willing to conform to anyone else's image of who or what she should be. Except God's, that is.
ISBN 1-59052-018-1

SOLD OUT, Chloe book two

Chloe and her fellow band members must sort out their lives as they become a hit in the local community. And after a talent scout from Nashville discovers the trio, all too soon their explosive musical ministry begins to encounter conflicts with family, so-called friends, and school. Exhilarated yet frustrated, Chloe puts her dream in God's hand and prays for Him to work out the details.
ISBN 1-59052-141-2

ROAD TRIP, Chloe book three

After signing with a major record company, Redemption's dreams are coming true. Chloe, Allie, and Laura begin their concert tour with the good-looking guys in the band Iron Cross. But as soon as the glitz and glamour wear off, the girls find life on the road a little overwhelming. Even rock-solid Laura appears to be feeling the stress—and Chloe isn't quite sure how to confront her about the growing signs of drug addiction...
ISBN 1-59052-142-0

FACE THE MUSIC, Chloe book four

Redemption has made it to the bestseller chart, but what Chloe and the girls need most is some downtime to sift through the usual high school stress with grades, friends, guys, and the prom. Chloe struggles to recover from a serious crush on the band leader of Iron Cross. Then just as an unexpected romance catches Redemption by surprise, Caitlin O'Conner—whose relationship with Josh is taking on a new dimension—joins the tour as a chaperone. Chloe's wild ride only speeds up, and this one-of-a-kind musician faces the fact that life may never be normal again.
ISBN 1-59052-241-9

Log onto www.DOATG.com

Lonely? Jealous? Hurt?
Melody Carlson addresses the
issues you face today.

The TrueColors Series

The TrueColors series addresses issues that most affect teen girls. By taking on these difficult topics without being phony or preachy, best-selling author Melody Carlson challenges you to stay true to who you are and what you believe.

Dark Blue
(Loneliness)
9781576835296

Faded Denim
(Eating Disorders)
9781576835371

Deep Green
(Jealousy)
9781576835302

Bright Purple
(Homosexuality)
9781576839508

Torch Red
(Sex)
9781576835319

Moon White
(Witchcraft)
9781576839515

Pitch Black
(Suicide)
9781576835326

Harsh Pink
(Popularity)
9781576839522

Burnt Orange
(Drinking)
9781576835333

Fool's Gold
(Materialism)
9781576835340

Blade Silver
(Cutting)
9781576835357

Bitter Rose
(Divorce)
9781576835364

9781576835296

9781576835319   9781576835302   9781576835364

To order copies, call NavPress at
1-800-366-7788 or log on to
www.NavPress.com.

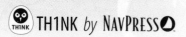

MY LIFE IS **TOUGHER** THAN MOST **PEOPLE REALIZE.**

I TRY TO
KEEP EVERYTHING
IN BALANCE:
FRIENDS, FAMILY, WORK,
SCHOOL, AND GOD.

IT'S NOT EASY.

I KNOW WHAT MY
PARENTS BELIEVE AND
WHAT MY PASTOR SAYS.

BUT IT'S NOT
ABOUT THEM.
IT'S ABOUT ME...

ISN'T IT TIME I
OWN MY FAITH?

THROUGH THICK AND THIN, KEEP YOUR HEARTS AT ATTENTION, IN
ADORATION BEFORE CHRIST, YOUR MASTER. BE READY TO SPEAK
UP AND TELL ANYONE WHO ASKS WHY YOU'RE LIVING THE WAY
YOU ARE, AND ALWAYS WITH THE UTMOST COURTESY. 1 PETER 3:15 (MSG)

www.navpress.com | 1-800-366-7788   THINK TH1NK *by* NAVPRESS